JULIA
ROSEINGRAVE

JULIA ROSEINGRAVE

MARJORIE BOWEN

Writing as

ROBERT PAYE

With an introduction by
JOHN C. TIBBETTS

This edition first published in 2025 by
The British Library
96 Euston Road
London NW1 2DB

Julia Roseingrave was first published in 1933 by Ernest Benn Ltd, London.

Introduction © 2025 John C. Tibbetts
Volume copyright © 2025 The British Library Board

Cataloguing in Publication Data
A catalogue record for this publication is available from the British Library

ISBN 978 0 7123 5532 2
e-ISBN 978 0 7123 6873 5

Cover and frontispiece design by Mauricio Villamayor
with illustration by Mag Ruhig
Text design and typesetting by Tetragon, London
Printed in England by CPI Group (UK) Ltd, Croydon, CR0 4YY

Eva Glyn writes escapist relationship-driven fiction with a kernel of truth at its heart. She loves to travel and finds inspiration in beautiful places and the stories they hide.

Set mainly in Croatia, her contemporary stories are more about friendship than romance, the coming together of people through shared interests, and the opportunity to make fresh starts in their lives. *The Santorini Writing Retreat* was her first book set in Greece.

In addition Eva has written two Second World War dual timeline romances, *An Island of Secrets* and *The Collaborator's Daughter*. All her books are published by One More Chapter, a division of HarperCollins.

Although she considers herself Welsh, Eva lives in Cornwall with the man she met and fell in love with more than thirty years ago. She also writes as Jane Cable.

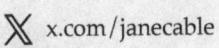

www.evaglynauthor.com

- x.com/janecable
- facebook.com/EvaGlynAuthor
- instagram.com/evaglynauthor
- bookbub.com/authors/eva-glyn

Also by Eva Glyn

The Missing Pieces of Us

The Olive Grove

An Island of Secrets

The Collaborator's Daughter

The Dubrovnik Book Club

The Santorini Writing Retreat

CONTENTS

Introduction	7
A Note from the Publisher	18
Story Sources	19
JULIA ROSEINGRAVE	21
SHORT STORIES	137
The Scoured Silk	139
Dark Ann	165
Hurry! Hurry!	186
Sheep's-head and Babylon	213
Red Champagne	227
The Sign-Painter and the Crystal Fishes	231

Drawing of Marjorie Bowen by John C. Tibbetts

INTRODUCTION

Marjorie Bowen: "An Enchanting Brewer of Dread"

> *My life was not set in pleasant places.*
> *In the jostle of the hundreds I always stood alone.*
> *I saw the devil look through many laughing faces*
> *And often felt his likeness rising in my own.*

This collection of some of the darker short stories of the writer known as "Marjorie Bowen"—one of her many pseudonyms—is welcome indeed, especially to those who have yet to discover the mysteries and magic of a body of work that earned her in her lifetime the sobriquet, "the enchanting brewer of dread".[*] For contemporary critics, scholars, and popular readers alike, attests her friend and sometime literary agent, Edward Wagenknecht, she was "one of the most gifted and amazingly fertile storytellers of our time."[†] Yet, her work has fallen into an undeserved obscurity since her death in 1952. This shortcoming is being redressed in several anthologies of her shorter stories, *Kecksies*, from Arkham House (1976); *Twilight*, from Ash-Tree Press (1998); *The Grey Chamber* and

---

[*] Sinclair Lewis, Foreword to *The Golden Violet* (New York: Press of the Readers Club, 1943), 6.

[†] Edward Wagenknecht, "Bowen, Preedy, Shearing & Co.: A Note in Memory and a Check List", in *Studies in English* (Boston University Press, 1957), 181.

INTRODUCTION

The Devil Snar'd, from Hippocampus Press (2021–2022); and the book you presently hold in your hands, which joins *The Haunted Vintage* (2024) in the British Library Tales of the Weird series.

Born Gabrielle Margaret Vere Campbell in 1885 on Hayling Island, Hampshire, she crowded into her lifetime, the many novels aside, an estimated 300 short stories and non-fiction articles in a variety of British and American magazines bearing familiar names like *Argosy*, *Harper's Monthly Magazine*, *The Strand*, *The Pall Mall Magazine*, *Hutchinson's Story Magazine*, *The Story-Teller*, *Ellery Queen's Mystery Magazine*; and less familiar names like *The Passing Show*, *Britannia and Eve*, *Colour*, *The Grand Magazine*, *The 20-Story Magazine*, and *The Regent Magazine*. Her readers may be forgiven for confusion about her identity. Her works appeared under a succession of pseudonyms, including "Joseph Shearing", "George Preedy", "Robert Paye", "John Winch", and "Margaret Long", and, yes, "Marjorie Bowen".[*] Her birth name was sometimes shortened to "Margaret Campbell". Her two memoirs, *The Debate Continues* and "Myself When Young", compounded the confusion. The latter appeared under *both* the names "Margaret Campbell" and "Marjorie Bowen"! Many names, she admitted with her customary sly ambivalence, but "they seemed rather to be fastened on me like a series of masks. I did not greatly care for any of them, nor does my other name—legally mine—appear to belong to me."[†] By

---

[*] She wrote more than ninety books as "Marjorie Bowen". "Marjorie" is the diminutive form of Margaret; "Bowen" was the name of her maternal great-grandfather.

[†] Marjorie Bowen, "Myself When Young", in Countess of Oxford, Asquith, ed., *Famous Women of Today* (London: Frederick Muller, 1938), 56.

the time she died in London in 1952, she left behind, she hinted, many stories as yet untold: "I am still absorbed in my own world of make-believe. I shall never tell all the tales, describe all the scenes and fantasies that possess me. I sometimes wonder how many will be untold when I am dead. And I regret the dreams that will die with me..."*

The story selection here captures the variety of themes and qualities and styles typical of her darker fantasies. "Few or none of these tales [are] pleasant," she once admitted—"magnanimous, heroic, lofty, but not pleasant, often full of dark and sinister shades. I found that, by writing of dark and gloomy subjects, I rid my mind of them."† Moreover, each one displays her mastery of vivid colour palettes and sensitivity to line and detail. Before she turned to a writing career, she had wanted to be a professional painter and designer. As a child, she scribbled characters and scenes on brown paper with chalks and charcoal. She haunted art galleries and thrilled to the drama and colour of the history paintings of Jean Léon Gerome, the rambunctious anecdotes of William Hogarth, the misty landscapes of William Turner and Caspar David Friedrich, the wicked satires of Honore Daumier, the Pagan visions of Giovanni Battista Tiepolo, etc. She studied briefly at the Slade School in London. But ultimately, her talents best lent themselves to her stories. She deployed her extensive knowledge of art history and her experience with paint and canvas, into ink and foolscap.

---

* Ibid, 56.

† Margaret Campbell, *The Debate Continues, Being the Autobiography of Marjorie Bowen* (London: William Heinemann, Ltd, 1939), 84–85.

For example, "Dark Ann", one of her most tenderly elegiac ghost stories, transpires among wintry landscapes evoked in the subdued range of muted blacks and whites characteristic of Caspar David Friedrich. Her mastery of the ghost story places her alongside her contemporaries M. R. James, Algernon Blackwood, and Walter de la Mare. Her ghosts, as one of her most empathetic and insightful critics, Jessica Amanda Salmonson, has noted, are generally not exterior manifestations: "Darkness reaches *outward* from within, rather than intruding from the outside... [They never let] the reader forget that she and we are each of us as much the perpetrators as the victims of inexplicable urges and activities."*

"Red Champagne" reveals her kinship with the close observation of scene, the taste for the absurd, and the bent for the anecdotal and grotesque of one of her favourite artists (about whom she wrote a critical study), William Hogarth. The story's account of a betrayed lover's grim retribution is a particularly fine example of the tradition of the *conte cruel*, those brief, tart, and cynical character sketches that carry a sting in the tail. No one—not even H. H. Munro ("Saki") and John Collier—crafted them better and in far greater numbers.

"The Scoured Silk" is a portrait of a marriage so stark and cruel that you may try in vain to forget its horrific conclusion. If any subject can be said to dominate Bowen's short stories, it is the marriage contract, fraught with mutual distrust, recriminations, and abuse. Doubtless stemming from her disastrous first marriage—related in bitter detail in several of her autobiographical narratives, notably,

---

* Jessica Amanda Salmonson, Introduction, *Twilight and Other Supernatural Romances* (Ashcroft, British Columbia: Ash-Tree Press, 1998), xxxvi.

Stinging Nettles (1923)—these brittle social satires were her own Balsacian "human comedy", where the pretensions of manners and morals are rudely punctured, and the veil of a romantic ideal is ruthlessly ripped away. The imagery and example of a satiric Daumier lithograph is never far away.

Bowen's humour and canny way with Scots dialect infuses the strange whimsies and hallucinatory visions of "Sheep's-head and Babylon". The dream sequences that beset the Reverend Zachary Barlas's visions of golden streets, towers, and erotic splendours evoke the processions of gods and goddesses, Pagans and Christians in the frescoes she enjoyed by Giovanni Battista Tiepolo. Indeed, Bowen's explorations of the pagan myths of England, Wales, Ireland, Scotland, Scandinavia, India, and Greece underpin many of her novels and stories. To play on the words of the temptress who appears to the Reverend Barlas: It is not so far, after all, from Drumknockie Manse to Babylon.

"The Sign-Painter and the Crystal Fishes" earns the distinction of a fable so enigmatic that it necessarily plays havoc with each reader's own interpretation. Synopsis is inadequate to convey its darkly picaresque quality: Characters die violently. Then they rise again. A boat carries its passengers to an unknown destination, while a one-eyed gypsy plays faro and sings to his companion: "There is no tomorrow for such as you. You had your neck broken an hour ago... Presently we will go home... your deal." The story's rude beauty is like a woodcut splashed with bloody colours. (It is a particular favourite of the present writer.)

"Hurry! Hurry!" is a swashbuckling narrative rooted in history. This pungent dramatisation of an assassination attempt against King Gustaf III of Sweden in 1792 serves as a preliminary sketch for the far more ambitious historical novel to come, *Nightcap and Plume* (1945). The vivid colour of courtly life and glittering masquerade balls resemble the vivid and gorgeously detailed history paintings of the nineteenth century French master, Jean-Léon Gerome. Since Bowen's breakthrough novel, *The Viper of Milan*, published in 1906 when she was still in her teens, her historical stories and novels dominated her entire output, from her first two story collections 1912 and 1917, *God's Playthings* and *Curious Happenings*, to the later procession of historical personages and events from the seventeenth and eighteenth-centuries, including Louis XIV, Richard III, William of Orange, and a host of celebrated women, including Mary Wollstonecraft. "I thought that the spirits of history were about me like pictures depicted in primary colours," she once wrote, "and the thought that they had once lived was enough to fill me with subdued satisfaction."[*]

Finally, *Julia Roseingrave*, the centrepiece of this book, demands special consideration. Witchcraft and sorcery, witches and warlocks, alchemical experiments were Bowen's lifelong preoccupations, and nowhere do they surface more vividly than in her short stories like the fanciful "'He Made a Woman—'" and the roaring melodrama of "One Remained Behind",[†] not to mention the novels *Black Magic* (1909) and *I Dwelt in High Places* (1933). The latter was a carefully researched dramatisation of the life and work of the Elizabethan astrologer and necromancer, John Dee. This was no affectation, no pandering for mere sensation. She cautioned

---

[*] Margaret Campbell, *The Debate Continues*, 32.

[†] These stories can be read in the Tales of the Weird volumes *Weird Woods* and *Doomed Romances* respectively.

against the outright dismissal of witchcraft in a scholarly article she published in *The Occult Review*, while researching Dee: "Who shall decide whether the explicable comes from the powers of Good or the powers of Evil?... Genius has never despised superstition, but used it with the finest effect and for the noblest purpose..."*

Julia Roseingrave was originally published in 1933 in a volume of that name and bearing the pseudonym, "Robert Paye". Julia may or may not be a witch. Certainly her powers of seduction seem preternatural, to say the least. She takes her place among the women who, as Edward Wagenknecht says, "if not a witch, [she] still tries their best to be one. [Such stories] come close to studying the effect of a deceptive belief in the supernatural upon a weak mind and of the fatality that follows upon disillusionment."† Her meeting with the handsome Sir William Notley, lately fled to his estate from some "bad business" in London, might be her ticket out of the rustic village, where she leads a blunted existence with her imbecile sister and sickly mother. She recruits two magician-accomplices in her scheme to seduce Sir William: Dr. Rowland is an alchemist, "whose mind and spirit dwelt much in other worlds... He was more used to the stars than to the earth, more at home in space than on solid ground," and old Goody Cloke is "a reputed witch who had a cottage down on the marshlands." The three are locked in an infernal rondelay of lust, greed, and betrayal. They exist in a world rendered indeterminate in space and time, hovering

---

* Marjorie Bowen, "Suspicion", *The Occult Review,* No. 32. Marjorie Bowen Papers, Beinecke Library, Yale, Box 22, 176–177.

† Edward Wagenknecht, "Marjorie Bowen", in *Seven Masters of Supernatural Fiction* (Westport, CT: Greenwood Press, 1991), 165.

between enchanted summer and imminent thunderstorm, all of it limned in "a subtle mist, light, yet not to be penetrated, as if mysteries were to be performed in Heaven, which must be veiled from the earth."

Bowen's prose here is gorgeous, intoxicating, sensuous. As is typical of her stories, events are surrounded at every turn by a profusion of blooms and exotic plants, intoxicating, heavily perfumed, poisonous. They recall the sumptuous English landscapes of Turner and Constable. Here, in one of the most enchanting scenes in all of Bowen, Sir William, who has been hitherto "weary of almost every delight that common joys and ordinary day could provide", finds himself in the moonstruck twilight of Ballote Wood where, he has been told, "a nymph or fairy or goddess walks there and bathes in the deep pool underneath the willow trees" (60):

> He waited but five minutes or so as he judged... when she appeared on the other side of the clearing. She was naked and held a long twist of black hair in her hand as she came lightly over the ground towards the pool... He stared, his heart panting, thick and frightening, believing he looked on something unearthly... She dipped her long limbs, and then sank beneath the water and began swimming across so that only her head and the black hair floating like a weed, showed...

And so on.

But to be sure, something is *wrong* here. Has he been drugged? A warning voice in his head urges: "Fly, you are in more danger now than you ever were in your life!" This liminal creature turns out to be none other than the all-too-real Julia Roseingrave, the "cool and self-possessed" inhabitant of a nearby cottage, whom he had first met on his arrival. But even then, in the plain light of day, her beauty had barely concealed "something not altogether pleasant in the steady look of her drowsy black eyes."

The machinery of spells, alchemical experiments, magical potions do not entirely disguise the fact that all these characters are themselves victims of their own devices. As Dr. Rowland declares to Sir William—in words that nicely describe one of the great themes in Bowen—"Have you become lunatic with fond and idle imaginings and unrestrained fancies? Do you not see that the net of the devil is about you? Even if you be something of a fiend yourself, a larger demon has you in his power."

Perhaps we can trace an affinity between the fictional Julia Roseingrave and Marjorie Bowen herself. Roseingrave embodies both the Apollonian sweetness and the Dionysian Furies that are the wellsprings of Bowen's art. Her capacities for rendering beautifully tender and sensitive stories about music, poetry, loss, and compassion are countered by others that are bluntly and horribly graphic. "As fast as the Mirthless Cosmic Jester poured misery into her," wrote Salmonson, "she made ink of bile to fill pages with dark visions, calamitous adventure, and cynical romances."[*] She takes her place as the literary heir of Mary Shelley. Like Shelley, she packed into the first decades of her life more turmoil, heartache, and literary

---

[*] Jessica Amanda Salmonson, "Rose Petals, Drops of Blood", in John C. Tibbetts, ed., *The Devil Snar'd* (New York: Hippocampus Press, 2023), 292. This essay, originally written for an unpublished volume of Bowen's stories, is published here for the first time with Ms Salmonson's permission.

accomplishment than most writers do in a lifetime. Like Shelley, she grew up, neglected, marginalised, and forced into her own modes of self-education and self-actualisation. Like Shelley, her first novel (*The Viper of Milan*) was greeted by critics incredulous at the precocity of female authorship. Like Shelley she was the sole support of her family as a professional writer. And both writers were in their respective lifetimes architects of what has been termed the "Female Gothic".[*] In sum, they were especially attuned to what Bowen called "The Music at Midnight", a darkling sympathy for the beauty of terror. "I interpret those words," she wrote in her autobiography, "as the courage to find beauty in dark places."[†]

After many years of reading and researching her life and works, I fall back in amazement at the strength, fierceness of purpose and indomitable integrity that seem to belie her personally mild manner and reclusive tendencies. A sceptic in matters of organised religion, a scholar of the Occult, a staunch social activist, and a defender of family and home, she was all those things—in short, a wholly admirable person, yes, but ultimately elusive, taunting us from behind the barriers of her contradictions and many pseudonyms. Perhaps at times she was a stranger to herself. "She cultivated her mind as far as her powers enabled her," she wrote, referring to herself in the third person. "Rationalism attracted and convinced her mind, but the heart has reasons that the mind knows not of, and she delighted in the mystics."[‡]

---

[*] See my essay, "The Music at Midnight: The Female Gothic of Mary Shelley and Marjorie Bowen", in *The Devil Snar'd*, 376–396.

[†] Margaret Campbell, *The Debate Continues,* 298.

[‡] Ibid, 293.

I can't pretend to any easy and startling insights into these mysteries. It's enough to luxuriate in their ambiguities. What I *do* know is what a pleasure it has been to revisit them in these pages and how grateful I am to have had the opportunity to do so from editor and publisher Jonny Davidson.

Let us sit back at last, raise a glass of ardent cordial in her honour, and turn the pages of this book...

> "I am Fantasy, day-dreaming and the unattainable. I beckon just round the corner where no one has been yet... I am all that is incredible yet pursued, all that is never credited, yet longed for."*

JOHN C. TIBBETTS is the author of *The Furies of Marjorie Bowen* (Jefferson, NC: McFarland, 2019); and editor of *Marjorie Bowen: The Grey Chamber, Stories and Essays* (Hippocampus Press, 2021) and *Marjorie Bowen: The Devil Snar'd, Novels, Appreciations, and Appendices* (Hippocampus Press, 2023). He dedicates this essay to Sharon and Mike Eden, the Keepers of the Flame.

---

*. [Writing as "George Preedy"] "Homage to the Unknown", in *Bagatelle* (New York: Dodd, Mead, 1931), 157.

A NOTE FROM THE PUBLISHER

The original short stories reprinted in the British Library Tales of the Weird series were written and published in a period ranging across the nineteenth and twentieth centuries. There are many elements of these stories which continue to entertain modern readers; however, in some cases there are also uses of language, instances of stereotyping and some attitudes expressed by narrators or characters which may not be endorsed by the publishing standards of today. We acknowledge therefore that some elements in the stories selected for reprinting may continue to make uncomfortable reading for some of our audience. With this series British Library Publishing aims to offer a new readership a chance to read some of the rare material of the British Library's collections in an affordable paperback format, to enjoy their merits and to look back into the worlds of the past two centuries as portrayed by their writers. It is not possible to separate these stories from the history of their writing and as such the following novel is presented as it was originally published with minor edits only, made for consistency of style and sense. We welcome feedback from our readers, which can be sent to the following address:

> British Library Publishing
> The British Library
> 96 Euston Road
> London, NW1 2DB
> United Kingdom

STORY SOURCES

Julia Roseingrave first published in Robert Paye (pseud.), *Julia Roseingrave* (London: Ernest Benn Ltd, 1933).

"The Scoured Silk" first published as "Crimes of Old London: The Scoured Silk" in *All-Story Weekly*, 8 June 1918 and collected in Marjorie Bowen, *Crimes of Old London* (London: Odhams Ltd, 1919).

"Dark Ann" first published in Marjorie Bowen, *Dark Ann and Other Stories* (London: John Lane The Bodley Head Ltd, 1927).

"Hurry! Hurry!" first published in George R. Preedy (pseud.), *The Knot Garden: Some Old Fancies Re-set* (London: The Bodley Head Ltd, 1933).

"Sheep's-head and Babylon" first published in *The Blue Magazine*, no. 60, June 1924 and collected in Marjorie Bowen, *Sheep's-head and Babylon: and Other Stories of Yesterday and To-day* (London: John Lane The Bodley Head Ltd, 1927).

"Red Champagne" first published in *Cassell's Weekly*, no. 25, 5 September 1923 and collected in George R. Preedy (pseud.), *The Knot Garden: Some Old Fancies Re-set* (London: The Bodley Head Ltd, 1933).

"The Sign-Painter and the Crystal Fishes" first published in *In a Good Cause: Stories and Verses on Behalf of the Hospital for Sick Children* (London: John Murray, 1909) and collected in Marjorie Bowen, *Curious Happenings* (London: Mills & Boon Ltd, 1917).

JULIA
ROSEINGRAVE

If I were to tell you a tale like this, would not you, who believe nothing, name it a "cock and bull story"?

I

Mrs. Barlow was extremely surprised to hear an iron tongue striking impatiently into the night, for she guessed this sound to be the clang of the great bell which hung over the main entrance to Holcot Grange; it was not the small bell which tinkled feebly over the side entrance that she and the other servants used.

The house had been uninhabited for two generations. It was well off the road nor was any traveller likely to pass... The imperious summons was repeated; Mrs. Barlow huddled on her clothes.

"I wonder when that sounded last?" she thought nervously, and, for company, she tried to rouse Grace, the maid who shared her room. But Grace was a country girl and slept as soundly as an exhausted animal. So Mrs. Barlow took up the lantern she had lit with trembling fingers. The moonlight was bright without, but she had to go through the shuttered portion of the house, along the left wing of Holcot Grange; she reached the front door and came out into the quadrangle as the bell rang a third time. The moonlight was very bright. The seven gables of the Grange were picked out sharply against a sky that dazzled with silver radiance. The moon itself hung above the old elms beyond, where the doves had made a deep cooing all day, but which now held only silence in their boughs.

Mrs. Barlow was not much comforted by this dazzle of moonlight which she always considered an unwholesome and unnatural illumination.

She hastened across the courtyard, keeping on her slippers with difficulty, and firmly holding the lit lantern, which gave a coarse yellow flame amid all the heavenly silver.

The entrance to Holcot Grange, which had not been opened for near half a century, was very magnificent. Two pillars held trophies of arms and garlands. The moonlight glistened on the white stone of these and made them appear as if they were covered with snow crystals, the gates between were of exquisitely hammered iron.

Through the sharp black design Mrs. Barlow could see a man holding a horse. The beast appeared weary, the man full of energy; with a useless gesture of impatience he struck with a glove on the iron grille and then, although he must have seen Mrs. Barlow approaching, pulled again at the iron chain connected with the great bell that hung to one side of the gates.

"I wonder how he's found it," grumbled Mrs. Barlow. She felt nervous and apprehensive of danger and called out (her own voice sounded thin and strange to her in the silence):

"Who are you, sir, and what do you want here? You must have sadly mistook your way!"

A man's voice that had the rough hoarseness which comes from one who has been silent for hours, replied:

"This is Holcot Grange, is it not?"

"Yes."

"Then it is the place I want." And, in an agony of impatience (with wrath, too, Mrs. Barlow feared), he added: "Whoever you are, open to me, and at once!"

"I must know your business," she trembled. She tried to make out his person and his features, but this was impossible, the moonlight was behind him, he was but a black shape. The animal, she could see, was weary, its head hung down and its motionless limbs and heaving body were steaming.

"I will tell you my business when I'm the other side of the gates."

Mrs. Barlow had been trained from a child to obey her superiors, and this man was plainly her superior. She had caught up her keys with her; she prided herself on never allowing these out of her sight, and among them, well polished and oiled but never used, was the key of the main gate.

She turned this stiffly in the ward with a trembling hand, while the man without continually urged haste, and as soon as the gate was forced on its rusty hinges, pushed through without ceremony. If Mrs. Barlow had been surprised by being roused in the middle of the night at a summons on the main gate of the deserted Grange, she was still more terribly surprised at the personage whom she had admitted, who was no less, her bulging eyes assured her, than the Devil himself.

The lantern fell from her hand, then crashed on the cobbles, and she would have shrieked had not the terrible guest at once put his hand over her mouth, bidding her, in the lewd and abominable terms she might have expected from such a character, to be silent.

"Who are you?" she stammered through his fingers, which was very foolish as she knew well enough that only one person could own such infernal insignia. Under his light, summer travelling cloak she could discern a tail which trailed on the ground as he walked. The hoofs she could not see, but then he wore hoggers, or riding boots, which might well have concealed such a deformity. The two points on his head which she had noticed with faint terror through the gate, she had thought and hoped to be feathers, or some outlandish ornamentation, but they were certainly horns.

For the rest, all she could see of his clothes was a tatter of red.

His face was smooth, hideous, expressionless, and a glittering yellow.

"Who am I?" he answered angrily, in reply to her quavering question, "I am your master. I have come home. Go in and prepare a bed and meal for me. And who is there to look after my horse?"

Mrs. Barlow, though ready to swoon with fright, contrived a defiance to the powers of darkness.

"You're no master of mine," she stammered. "I've been a God-fearing Christian ever since I could talk."

He had taken his hand from her mouth and stared at her with those glassy, unnatural eyes in such a threatening fashion that she began to moan, and added in a tone of complete surrender:

"I'll rouse Jack and tell him to look after your horse."

"I perceive you are a fool," he answered, "and that nothing is to be got from you," he then turned away and walked towards the house.

Mrs. Barlow stared after him, black and red in the moonlight as he crossed the quadrangle. She had left the great front doors open behind her and he passed into the house and closed them.

"Oh dear, oh Lord, I have let the Devil into the house! The Devil has shut himself into the house!" whimpered Mrs. Barlow.

Great as was this misfortune, she felt a certain relief at being rid of his actual presence, and the sight of the poor tired horse standing dejectedly beyond the gates, restored a little of her common sense and her courage. If the rider had come from the infernal regions, the horse at least seemed ordinary flesh and blood.

Mrs. Barlow went out of the gates that she had never passed through before, closed them behind her, and taking the bridle of the weary animal led it round the Grange to the side gate, passed through this postern into the parts familiar to herself where she lived with her fellow servants, Grace and Jenny, in an irregular pile of outbuildings which had been built on the back of the Grange. There were stables here and the stable boy slept above those occupied by the two horses used by the menservants.

With tears and cries and lamentations Mrs. Barlow roused this youth, who presently came down the ladder, dragging on his smock and pulling at the straps of his leggings, with straw in his hair and horror in his eyes, for Mrs. Barlow kept on repeating that the Devil had gone into the Grange, she had let him in with her own hand—the Devil and no one else, tail and horns and all...

But the boy looked at the horse.

"That's an ordinary animal," he said, "and has been ridden fast and bad and a good many miles too."

"Well, I hope," cried Mrs. Barlow, "that Hell is a long way off! I wouldn't like to think it were just round the corner."

"But it's not much of a bit of horseflesh for the Devil to be riding," remarked Jack with slow shrewdness. "Why, it's just an ordinary post hack, hired at some stage inn."

"I don't care what it is, the Devil was riding it and he's gone into the house!"

"Gone into the Grange!"

The youth was plainly awed. Neither he nor Mrs. Barlow could remember when anyone had been in the Grange before, save the servants when they went to clean and repair.

"Yes, he went into the Grange, through the great gate and through the front door, and he's there now. You had better take up a lantern and come with me, Jack, and look for him, from room to room. It's our plain duty to do so."

But the boy never gave this proposal even a second's consideration. He shook his head resolutely.

"I'll look after the horse, but I won't come into the Grange with you, Mrs. Barlow, not if it meant losing my place."

The housekeeper wrung her hands, torn between a very reasonable and bitter fear and a keen, honest sense of duty.

"What shall I do?" she kept saying in a foolish fashion, her goggling eyes staring at the boy, as he put the horse in the stable and unharnessed it.

"If I were you I'd go and ask the advice of Miss Julia Roseingrave," suggested the lad. "She's clever. She'll be able to tell you if you're dreaming, or if it's all just moonshine, and I shouldn't be surprised if she didn't mind going with you and searching over the Grange."

With that, Jack, grinning, closed the stable door.

Mrs. Barlow followed his advice. She had a great respect both for the courage and the judgment of Miss Julia Roseingrave.

So she set off, very panting and exhausted, along the path under the chestnut trees to the Dower House where Miss Roseingrave lived with her mother and her sister Phœbe. The housekeeper had begun to hope by now that she might have been dreaming or suffering from some horrible hallucination. The grinning incredulity of Jack had somewhat restored her equanimity. At the same time Jack had refused to go into the Grange with her, and as a proof that something tangible had arrived that night there was the exhausted, sweating horse.

The estate was small. The Dower House was not much more than a large cottage, nor was it far from the Grange. The familiar sight of the plain, brick front, with honeysuckles growing over the porch, and the pretty rose-pink curtains showing in the moonlight gave Mrs. Barlow fresh heart.

She knocked at the door, and an upper window was instantly opened. Julia Roseingrave was always on the alert, and her neat, graceful head and shoulders looked out, as her dark eyes were turned on Mrs. Barlow.

"Why, Mrs. Barlow! At this time of night? It is very late, is it not?"

"Oh, Miss Julia, if you would come down and allow me to speak to you!"

"Certainly, I shall come down. But is it so important? Cannot you tell me now?"

"It's only this," said poor Mrs. Barlow, "I believe I've let the Devil into the Grange."

Julia Roseingrave laughed.

"Indeed Mrs. Barlow, that would be very interesting, after you have had no company for so long to be thus honoured! Pray, tell me all about it."

"Oh, Miss Julia, I knew you would mock me, but someone came up tonight, there's his horse in the stable now and young Jack attending to it. And I opened the great gates that have never been opened before. At least, not that I can remember, nor anyone else that I know, and the front door, too, and he passed straight in."

"Some traveller," said Miss Julia coolly. "Don't talk too much and too loud, Mrs. Barlow, you will wake my mother. I shall be down directly."

The housekeeper was instantly silent, she was rather afraid of Miss Julia, but she admired and respected her very much.

In a very short while Miss Julia was down and had opened the door. She held a candle in her hand which showed her very neatly arrayed in a dimity gown, her hair smoothly combed, her buckled shoes on her feet; she seemed never to be taken by surprise. Mrs. Barlow followed her into the small parlour where everything was fair and orderly.

"Now, Mrs. Barlow, pray tell me this strange tale."

Mrs. Barlow obeyed, and when she had finished her breathless recital, Miss Julia did not laugh or mock, but said, pleasantly:

"It is clear that someone has gone into the Grange, and someone who has no business to be there. Of course, it is nonsense about it being the Devil, and, of course, we must go and see who it is. You say that Jack would not go, and of course neither of the maids would. And there's nobody else, is there?"

Mrs. Barlow shook her head. There would be nobody else at Holcot Grange till the morning, when the gardener and two other men who worked there would come up from the village for their day's work.

"Well, I shall go," said Julia Roseingrave, "if you will stay here, Mrs. Barlow, in case my mother or my sister wake. You know that they must never be left alone."

Mrs. Barlow knew. Miss Julia's mother was a paralytic, and her sister Phœbe was an imbecile. But she made a protest against the young woman undertaking such a dangerous expedition as that she proposed, to the deserted Grange where the Devil had certainly taken up his night's lodging. But her protests were not very vehement, for she really thought this a good solution of the problem. She did not want to go to the Grange herself, she did not know anybody else who would go, and yet she was very willing to have the mystery solved as soon as possible. She also knew that Julia Roseingrave was completely without fear; never had she seen her in the least discomposed nor put out by any person, so she agreed to stay with the two invalids in the Dower House while Julia Roseingrave, putting a light shawl over her shoulders and taking Mrs. Barlow's keys in her hand, set off through the moonlight under the chestnut trees towards the Grange.

She could have found her way there in the dark, for she had been a very young child when she had first come to live at the Dower House, and she was now a woman of twenty-seven.

As she proceeded directly, but without haste, on this strange errand, she turned over in her mind the nonsensical story of the housekeeper, which she thought the more striking, because she had always found the woman sensible and quiet, not given to either hysterics or romancing. Some traveller, she decided, whose fantastic appearance had deceived the good woman... "But why should there be a traveller going past Holcot Grange?—for the road leads nowhere, and who could have had the impertinence to force his way in thus without an explanation?... leaving poor Mrs. Barlow in such a fright."

The housekeeper's last injunction to her, whispered from under the honeysuckle-leaved porch of the Dower House had been that she must surely rouse Jack or get Grace or the other maid to go with her for company, but Miss Julia Roseingrave never gave this advice a thought. She did not wish to be embarrassed by the company of fools or rustics. The adventure was in her own hands, where she wished to keep it. She was indeed afraid of nothing.

"The house is under a curse," Mrs. Barlow had quavered.

Julia Roseingrave was not afraid of that menace either. The fancy also took her to enter the Grange by the front entrance. She had been into the house but very seldom, and only on those occasions when the servants were cleaning. There had been always a sort of understanding that she was not to go into the house, and Mrs. Barlow had tacitly given her to understand that she would not very readily give her the keys. So there were many rooms and many things in the house which Miss Julia Roseingrave had never seen and which she had a rather lively curiosity to see. It pleased her, too, to enter by the great gates which she had always seen chained and then through the big main doors always kept closed. The house was not very large nor very magnificent, but it was the largest and most magnificent that she had ever seen. For years she had envied the owner of Holcot Grange.

So, skirting the outbuildings where the servants lodged, the stables and, beyond, the disused chapel, she went leisurely round to the front of the house. The iron gates were closed. She unlocked them with a pleasurable sensation of power and passed into the moonlit quadrangle. The whole house was clear before her and she studied it intently. There was no light in any of the windows; the gables rose sharply against the moonlight-filled sky. A faint night breeze rustled in the tops of the elms; her own shadow and the design of the gate lay black before her on the cobbles, which were bleached to the look of marble by the moonlight.

No house could have seemed more blank and silent than did the Grange. "The foolish woman imagined it all," thought Julia Roseingrave with a feeling of disappointment.

She went up to the front door and after some difficulty found the right key and entered. Then in the hall she lit the candle, on the plain stick, that she had brought with her... the stairs were directly before her; leading up into darkness.

She listened. There was no sound, except, after she had stood still a considerable while, the scuttle of a mouse in the wainscoting.

"If there were indeed anyone here and he is as tired as his horse is said to be, he would have gone upstairs to rest, I suppose."

And resolutely holding her candle aloft Miss Julia Roseingrave mounted the stairs.

"The Devil, I suppose, would choose the finest apartments."

She remembered the largest bedroom that had been always used by the master of Holcot Grange, when it had had a master. She turned to that and opened the door.

The room was fully furnished, and like the rest of the house kept in tolerable repair; Mrs. Barlow fulfilled her duties conscientiously; the two maids had nothing else to do but to keep repaired, darned and cleaned, the hangings and the furniture of the deserted house.

Shielding her light with a delicate hand Julia Roseingrave entered the room and softly closed the door behind her. There were long curtains of green rep to the bed and these were half pulled back. The shutters were closed and there was no sign of disarray in the room, but the young woman sensed that someone was lying in the bed.

With a steady hand she pulled back the sage-green curtains, and saw extended there in a deep slumber, the figure that had so affrighted Mrs. Barlow—a man in a tattered carnival dress of scarlet was lying stretched on the hangings which Mrs. Barlow kept rolled up in the bed. The tufted tail which the housekeeper had found so affrighting now looked ridiculous and even pitiful, trailing across the relaxed limbs.

The man had not even pulled off his boots. His dusty cloak still hung from his shoulders and he had loosened but not removed a mask of light gilded wood with holes for lips and eyes, and which still partially covered his face—a hood with crumpled cardboard horns lay beneath his head.

Julia Roseingrave stared at this stranger in a rapt curiosity. She wondered where he could have come from... For miles around, the monotonous countryside afforded no more than a few sheep farms. She knew of no house where the people were rich enough and idle enough to amuse themselves by dressing up as devils.

With a delicate and adroit hand she pulled aside the mask, and looked at the stranger's features. His face was peculiar and to some tastes handsome. In his slumber it twitched as if in the spasm of some half-spent passion or the feverish dreams of over-exhaustion. He was dark, and his curls, very rich and full, were pressed into the hood with the trumpery cardboard horns. He did not look the thoughtless fool that his disguise and his strange entrance to Holcot Grange, might have shown him to be.

Miss Julia Roseingrave supposed that he was drunk. He was powerful and a small sword and a case of travelling pistols lay beside him on the bed. She knew it might very likely be dangerous to rouse him, but she did not hesitate.

Carefully placing her candle on a tall table by the bedside she bent over the sleeper, and, using more force than her fine hands seemed capable of, took him by the shoulders, commanding him, at the same time, in a low, tense voice, to wake up and tell her his business in Holcot Grange.

After a while he did stir, with a sigh and a groan as one who surrenders with reluctance a hard-won repose. She continued to shake him and adjure him. He sat up in the bed and opened his eyes which were swollen and bloodshot, but of a deep blue that she instantly admired.

"Who are you? Perhaps you do not even know who you are?" she asked, "and what are you doing here? You frightened poor Mrs. Barlow, the housekeeper, very much with your foolish costume, and your forcing of your way here in the middle of the night."

He set his teeth at her with a mechanical ferocity, not meant, she thought, for her at all, but for some personage out of the episode which had sent him flying through the dark to shelter.

"Do not be foolish," she said coldly, "explain yourself. This is not an inn nor the house of any friend of yours."

He seemed, by then, to have some little sense of his situation. He looked at the young woman and then beyond her at as much of the room as the candle light allowed him to see.

"To whom does this house belong?" he asked, and his voice, though still hoarse, was steady. She believed that she had made a mistake when she had assumed him to be drunk for the man seemed sober enough.

"The house belongs to Sir William Notley," she said. "He has never been here in all his life. No, nor his father, neither. Sir William has many finer and larger estates."

The stranger smiled. He seemed now to be alert. Miss Julia Roseingrave liked the way in which he was studying her and her neat charms. To allow him to prolong his scrutiny, she lengthened her conversation, telling him unnecessarily:

"Sir William never comes here. He is a very wealthy man. This place is lonely, desolate, old-fashioned, but he pays to have it kept up. It is supposed to be under a curse, nobody lives in it at all. I don't think till Mrs. Barlow, in her fright, opened to you tonight, that the front door and gates have been unlocked for half a century."

Then, her curiosity proving stronger than the pleasure she found in the stare of the handsome young man, she asked quickly:

"Who are you and where did you come from? I don't know anyone for miles round here who would be holding carnival!"

"Pray," said he, rising stiffly to his feet as if he suddenly remembered some courtesy, "who are you thus to question me?"

"Well, if you want to know that, I'm Julia Roseingrave."

"And what right have you in this house which you say the owner has not inhabited for all his life?"

"I live in the Dower House," said Miss Roseingrave, "with my mother and my sister. My mother is a distant cousin of Sir William's father. It was he, of his charity, when we were quite ruined, who allowed us the Dower House. Sir William has not withdrawn that favour, so there we have been for twenty years. Tonight, Mrs. Barlow, that is the housekeeper who admitted you, came running to me to tell me she had let the Devil into Holcot Grange."

"And you came by yourself to investigate if that were true or no?"

"Why, certainly. Do you think we get so many excitements here that I could let that one pass?"

The young man leant against the bed pillar. His interest in her, which seemed to have flared up so suddenly, had suddenly sunk down; he was again overpowered by fatigue. He seemed indeed near swooning.

"I will see you in the morning," he said. "Pray do me the kindness to give orders from me to that foolish woman who admitted me, that the house is to be opened and aired. The house is mine though I have never been here before."

"You are Sir William Notley?" she asked very quick and peering.

"I am he, Miss Roseingrave, and I shall stay here for a while. I have a good reason for that and a good reason for coming here suddenly. Good night, cousin."

Then he threw himself down again on the rolled up coverlet, smiling in his tattered devil's finery. The young woman thought instantly:

"Mr. Morley, the steward, who lives over at Griffinshaws, will know if this is he or no. Meanwhile it were best that I accepted his tale."

So she said, still composed, but pale:

"It is a very strange home-coming, Sir William, and you must forgive us if we mistook you. Will you not have another bed prepared, it can be done in a little while?"

"I have ridden from London, only stopping to change horses, and I could sleep on a board."

"Good night, then, cousin, I will see you, perhaps, in the morning."

She took up her candle daintily and left him.

In this strange fashion Miss Julia Roseingrave and Sir William Notley first met.

II

When the young man woke it was well past noon on a perfect summer day and the room full of a dull brownish light which filtered through the joints, in the shutters in each of which blazed a small mock sun through the round aperture in the wood.

Sir William looked at his strange bed, his pillow of rolled tapestries, his mattress of grey serges and holland covers, and sat up, pulled aside the sage-green curtains and stared about him. He could not for a while, remember where he was, but he remembered perfectly where he had come from—the masquerade, the brawl, the murder, the flight into the night, the advice given by the friend who had clung to his bridle even as he was starting.

"Why don't you go to Holcot Grange? Nobody will look for you there! You will be your own master. It will blow over in a week or so."

Yes, he could remember that, and the ride, and the change of horses at the post-house... they had been very glad to take the beautiful but exhausted horse from the young gentleman in his carnival dress who was riding, he said, for a wager, and to give him in exchange the post hack which had brought him to Holcot Grange...

Holcot Grange! That, then, was where he was now...

He sat up and put his aching head into his hands, and remembered the woman who had roused him in the middle of the night.

She, surely, was a dream, but he recalled the name she had given him—Julia Roseingrave—an extraordinary name. Surely he had heard it before? She had been unlike any other woman he had ever seen, and his fine taste in gallantry dwelt on her with zest. So cool and self-possessed she was, so dark of hair and eye, and yet so pale of skin, very erect, neat figured and small boned, with hands that were very delicate and yet strong enough to rouse him by shaking his shoulder. He could recall her dress laced so tightly round the waist... little sprigs of roses all over it. There had been something not altogether pleasant in the steady look of her drowsy black eyes. She had been readier with her speech than he cared for in a woman. What had the woman been like for whom that sudden blood had flown at the masquerade? He could scarcely remember.

He rose and looked down with disgust at the painted mask lying on the bed, and then at his own ragged and tattered scarlet suit, the fantastic boots of painted leather; he did not believe that he would ever wear a masquerade dress again. Never in his life before had he been without a body servant. He stood helpless, without clothes, without service, and then impatiently pulled off the tawdry scarlet finery, the gaudy, dusty boots and stood in shirt, breeches and stockings.

He opened the shutters and the strong sweetness of the day overpowered him.

"Am I master of this place? I never saw anything so alien."

He found a bell rope and pulled it, and when Mrs. Barlow, at once suspicious and deferential, overawed and incredulous, came, he desired her to send someone at once to Griffinshaws, to fetch the steward, Mr. Morley he believed the name was—indeed, he had almost forgotten that...

III

Miss Roseingrave was a very self-contained character and led a reserved life. She always disdained to gossip with the servants at the Grange or to make any acquaintance with the neighbouring farmers; those who had timidly endeavoured to solicit her friendship had received sharp rebuffs. Even the strange home-coming of Sir William Notley did not induce her to lower her pride so far as to go up to the Grange and ask Mrs. Barlow for news.

When, in last night's moonlight, she had returned home she had merely gone to the little kitchen where the housekeeper sat gibbering and praying and said coldly:

"Mrs. Barlow, you are a very foolish woman. It is your master come home—Sir William himself—or else some acquaintance of his making a clever imposture. Mr. Morley of Griffinshaws will soon set us aright on that matter, but as for the Devil," the young woman had laughed contemptuously, "why, I wonder that those tawdry bits so deceived you!" And then, without waiting for the abashed woman to reply with exclamations of doubt and astonishment, she had blown out her candle and ascended, by the light of the moon to her own room, still filled with silver light.

On the next hot, quiet day she had gone decorously about her duties. There were plenty of these in the Dower House, for though it was but small it was elaborately furnished and Miss Roseingrave had no assistance beyond that of Mother Cloke, a reputed witch who had a cottage down on the marshlands; she would work for none other than Miss Roseingrave, nor would Miss Roseingrave employ any other woman. She disdained to give any explanation for this peculiar choice, for there was many a hard-working, lusty girl who would have been glad of the work at the Dower House; she might have had her choice of many servants, but would have none other than the gnarled Mother Cloke of dubious reputation.

No doubt this association helped to give a slightly sinister air to Miss Roseingrave's retirement at the Dower House. Mrs. Barlow and the other servants who looked after the Grange, the tenants of the scattered sheep farms, the shepherds who tended their flocks in the wide fields sloping to the marsh, the village folk, all thought with a certain awe, of the young woman who lived in the Dower House amid the chestnut trees of the great park with her imbecile sister and her paralysed mother and only Mother Cloke to help her nurse these two piteous invalids, for Phœbe was sickly as well as feeble-minded, and often came near to dying.

It was known that the Roseingraves had the Dower House through the charity of the late Sir William and that they were in some way his relatives, but their history was vague in the minds of their simple neighbours. Mrs. Roseingrave, though now stiff and distorted by her disease, yet bore the remains of considerable beauty, and the tale went that she had been a *belle* and well dowered, too, from a fine family; she had run away with a poor musician who had afterwards gone mad and left her penniless, and only through her desperate appeal to her cousin, the late Sir William, had she and her two daughters found this asylum in their utmost distress.

However this might be, Miss Roseingrave never spoke of her past nor of her mother's story, nor did any relatives of her father's family ever come to visit them, nor the mail-coach ever leave letters for them at the "Ewe and Lamb." They had lived isolated in the park of the deserted Grange for twenty years. Their visitors were few; sometimes the Vicar rather timidly made his way into the park and drank a dish of tea with Miss Julia. She did not encourage this courtesy and was seldom seen at the church, though she professed a cold orthodoxy. She had a valid excuse for her neglect, in the charge of her afflicted relatives.

Sometimes, too, Dr. Rowland would come to the Dower House, and he seemed more after Miss Julia's mind. He was learned and a great scholar and might have done well for himself in the City, but preferred a philosophic peace.

He was a man of great mental energy and all his activities were turned inward, for outwardly he led an eventless life. His mind and his spirit dwelt much in other worlds, and he was accused of magical experiments and crystal gazing and even of some obscure partnership with Mother Cloke, whose knowledge of natural forces he had often declared to be extraordinary.

But Doctor Rowland lived far away from Holcot Grange and was much absorbed in his own speculations and experiments, so his visits, therefore, to Miss Julia Roseingrave, were rare.

One other acquaintance this lady had who might be considered of her own rank, that was Mr. Morley, steward of Holcot, who lived at Griffinshaws. He was a middle-aged man, robust, and not uncomely. Five years before he had had the daring to offer himself as a suitor for the hand of the dark young woman. He was so sincere in his passion, which took more the form of a fascination than an affection, that he, practical and businesslike as he was, had been prepared to waive the question of the young lady's dowry. He understood that she lived on a mere pittance and even that, such as it was, would have to be reserved for her helpless mother and sister. But she had refused him with sharp contempt, and when he, being really involved in the affair, had overlooked her insults and still pressed his suit, she took him into the Dower House and showed him her mother, lying rigid on a couch, and her sister drolling by the window and said to him with a fine curl of her arched upper lip: "Are you willing to take these too, with you, till one of us, you or I, die? As for the insane, Dr. Rowland tells me they will live very long."

Then Mr. Morley had gone away without a word and a twelve-month after had married a farmer's daughter who made him happy. His feelings for Miss Julia Roseingrave had had a curious reaction, he now never saw her without feeling glad that he had not married her, yet, as far as her beauty went, she had improved with the years. She was now a rare creature, of such uncommon graces that they were not rightly to be valued by the rustics among whom she lived.

The day after the coming of Sir William Notley to Holcot Grange, Mr. Morley, who had, early in the day, been summoned to the house, chose to return through the park, and rode his horse slowly past the Dower House. He was not above the pleasure of giving and receiving news, and Mrs. Barlow had told him of the part Miss Roseingrave had played last night. He was not deceived in his expectation that she would be waiting for him, she must have been listening for the sound of his horse's hoofs, for by the time he reached the Dower House she was standing under the honeysuckle on the porch.

Mr. Morley looked at her with a curious sense of the emptiness and deadness of the little house behind. Her alert and vivid vitality was like a tiny flame in a dark lantern. The coral horns of the honeysuckle waved above her dark hair and she was wiping, on a small square of muslin, her fingers, stained from plucking currants.

"I thought you would come this way," she smiled. "You want to speak to me about last night, I suppose."

Mr. Morley, leaning good-humouredly from his saddle, tried to turn this about.

"I thought you would want to know the news, Miss Roseingrave."

But her indifference was not to be pierced.

"Oh, I care very little. You may ride on if you will."

So then he had to surrender, for he was eager to tell someone of his interview with Sir William, and who else was there to tell besides Miss Julia Roseingrave? His own wife would be totally disinterested. She was absorbed, dear, pretty Priscilla, as a good kind woman should be, in the two babies, and her house.

"It is Sir William in very truth, though I believe, Miss Julia, last night you doubted it. It was very courageous of you to go up there alone after Mrs. Barlow's crazy story of the Devil."

"Why was it courageous, since the story was so crazy?" she countered, "and I did believe it was Sir William. Who else could have known the place and come in with such effrontery?" Then lowering her voice she added cunningly: "What has he done?"

"Why, what should he have done?" replied Mr. Morley, uncomfortably. "He had a whim to come here, I suppose. It is one of his properties that he has never visited before."

"And would not have visited now," said Miss Roseingrave, "had he not had a good reason. Do you think, Mr. Morley, that he would have come here to make your acquaintance or mine?"

"It would be only natural, Miss Roseingrave, that he should wish to see the place, which, after all, is a property of considerable value, and has been well and carefully kept up."

"To come here like that at dead of night in a stupid carnival dress, masked, and on a sweating post-horse!"

The steward shrugged before her cool contempt.

"Well, if Sir William has his story he does not tell it to me. He said he was here for several months, for the full summer, he thought. That he was sick of town ways and rioting; he gave me to understand that he had not a great deal of money, but had gambled away whole estates and sold others and was by no means the rich man we still suppose him."

"He looked," remarked Miss Roseingrave dryly, "that manner of fool."

"Fool, I don't think he is," said Mr. Morley, "but merely a young fashionable who must go the way of his time and his set. He told me there was something he wished to do, for which he must have privacy. To write a book or make some chemical experiment, as I suppose. No doubt it is but a whim of one who can afford to indulge whims."

"No doubt," echoed Miss Julia Roseingrave. "I do not suppose he will be here for longer than a short time. The rest of the summer shall we say? Six weeks, two months?"

"His servant," said the steward, "is coming today with some of his effects. At present he has nothing to wear but my brown kersey suit he begged me to bring along."

"You are sure that it is Sir William Notley?" asked Miss Roseingrave. She came from under the waving shadows of the honeysuckle and approached Mr. Morley's side. From the Dower

House came the sudden sound of the idiot girl singing in a thin, broken voice.

"Yes, it is Sir William," said Mr. Morley. "I have never seen him before, but his conversation proves that he is no impostor."

"Where did he come from?" asked the young lady. Her slender, cool fingers, which smelt of currant leaves, patted the glossy neck of the bay horse.

"I believe he came from London." Mr. Morley could not resist gossiping. He lowered his voice, carefully, however; he thought it was not altogether wise, even in the depths of the park, to be turning tales of his master on whom his livelihood depended, over his tongue. "And I believe, Miss Julia, that there was some trouble. Some riot or brawl, or maybe a *duello*, for he had certainly ridden fast, and it was a strange dress to ride in."

"How did he get through the turnpikes?"

"By talking, I suppose, of a wager."

"What manner of man do you suppose him to be, Mr. Morley?"

And Julia Roseingrave raised her dark eyes that were full of a deep lustre like a flame reflected in a stone of polished jet, to the good-natured, comely face of the steward.

"I could not judge much in a short interview, Madam Julia, but he seemed to me to be rather a fantastical kind of a fellow, full of odd notions and whims and who must be ever experimenting. He thinks that he will have a new experience at Holcot Grange such as he has reach of in poems writ by men who have never been out of a town, of neat handed Phillis, and curds and whey, lowing herds and bowls of cream and perpetual peace."

"There is all that here," smiled Miss Julia. "Give my duty to your wife."

Thus, with a nod and a smile, as if she dismissed an inferior, Miss Julia returned to the Dower House. She had scarcely closed the door behind her before the wild songs of the idiot girl ceased.

Mr. Morley rode on his way with a faint sense of uneasiness, which never failed to touch him after he had encountered Miss Roseingrave. He pondered a little over her name—a rose-in-a-grave—when he had first seen her he had thought it should be rather rose-in-leaf, or rose-in-bloom, but now he did rather think of her as a rose shut into a grave; the grave of that lonely house, with those two people who lived their death in life around her.

Sir William Notley had asked him questions of Miss Roseingrave, and he, Jonathan Morley, had answered them with some embarrassment.

What was there to say of her? She was much respected and admired.

By whom?

By simple rustics who rather feared her reserve and pride.

"Why does she continue to live there?" Sir William had asked impatiently. "Why did she come to look at me last night? That was a strange thing to do."

Then Mr. Morley had found himself saying, though he had not meant to admit as much:

"She is a strange woman."

To which remark the young baronet had replied with a certain exasperation:

"Bah! There is no such thing as a strange woman. I have met a fair number, Mr. Morley, but look you, there were none of them strange, though many of them affected to be thought so."

IV

When Mother Cloke came up that evening to the Dower House to redress Mrs. Roseingrave's bed and set all the house in order for the night and the morrow, Miss Julia gave her a large glass of damson wine, a privilege that the old woman only had when Miss Julia was in a good humour or required some favour.

Mother Cloke, like many another wise, learned and laborious person, remained very poor. She would not work for any save Miss Julia, and the peasants were frightened to go near her, even though they often greatly longed to ask her for a potion or to implore her to weave a spell. She did a little trade in face washes and balms, and unguents, but this brought her in but a few pence.

She could not often afford such luxuries as a large glass of wine.

Miss Roseingrave watched her as she drank, seated in the neat kitchen, where everything was shining and furbished, and a blue bowl lavishly filled with roses stood on the scrubbed oak table.

Mother Cloke was a pale, meek looking woman, in colouring like a sandy cat. She always wore a mutch bonnet and a tippet of stiff white linen and a skirt of grey cotton damask. She was clean in her person, too, which was one reason why Miss Roseingrave employed her. Her clothes and her hands always had a faint perfume from the herbs that she so constantly touched.

"I wish," said Miss Roseingrave, watching the old woman relish gratefully the thick purple liquid, "that you really were a witch,

Mother Cloke, and that some of your herbs had the virtues that the rustics think they have."

"And what would you want of me, my dear, if that were true?" asked Mother Cloke pleasantly. She had a soft, pleasant voice that seemed cultured above her station.

"I would ask you for a love potion."

"And I have been asked for that often enough." The herb woman nodded above her wine. "But what need would you have, Madame Julia, for such a thing?"

"Why should I not have need of it?"

The young woman drew her thick black brows together in a heavy frown.

"There is never a man round here worth your pains, Madame Julia."

"The young squire came home last night, Mrs. Cloke, and if you had such a potion as I have mentioned I would take it up to him and see that Mrs. Barlow mixed it with his caudle."

"Is he, then, so brave and goodly, Madame Julia?"

"As to that, nothing much. As far as I marked him, but an ordinary kind of man. But I think of his place and his power, Mrs. Cloke, and his parks and his houses, and how pleasantly gorgeous the world might be for the woman who was his wife."

Miss Roseingrave turned about and stirred the pap for her mother that was cooking in a small pot on the little fire which was gathered to one corner of the hearth.

Mother Cloke finished the last drop of the damson wine and said:

"I did not think you were ambitious, Madame Julia, you have stayed here so long and so patiently."

"When one has no hope one is patient."

"And have you now a little hope, Miss Roseingrave?"

The young woman rose from her task; the spoon on which the milk steamed was still in her hand. She looked very thin in her tight-laced cotton gown and swayed like a willow herb in the breeze as she spoke. She was moved, it seemed, by some considerable emotion.

"Look you, Mother Cloke, surely you know of something which the ignorant call a love potion, that confuses the senses and raises the appetite and might make this man desire me, seeing there is no other woman within his reach, nor like to be these many weeks, save sluts, at whom I am sure he would not look."

Mother Cloke shook her head and pursed her lips.

"I have never meddled in such matters," she muttered. "I can tell you many secrets, and have already told you a few, Madam Julia, for easing the stomach and the head, for beautifying the complexion, stopping the bleeding of green wounds, even for checking the ague and driving away a mad fit, for giving sleep and raising the spirits; but as for love potions, could I have discovered them, I should have been a rich woman long ago." She added on a whistling sigh: "Poisons were ever easy to find, but everything else is difficult."

Miss Roseingrave looked angry.

"I have never been discontented till now," she said. "But he is a fool who does not take an opportunity when it comes his way."

"Take it by natural means," suggested the old woman uneasily. "No pretty lady should need to ask for the help of spells."

"I want but a charm to bring him here," muttered Julia Roseingrave. "Once I could see him and frequently, the thing were done, as I take it. How can I go up to the Grange without a sacrifice of my pride and making a mockery of myself to the servants?"

"As to that," said Mother Cloke, setting the tray for the invalid woman, "I daresay I can contrive it and in a lawful manner."

V

For several days after his coming to Holcot Grange, Sir William lay on his bed, which Mrs. Barlow had made very comfortable with clean sheets and soft coverlets, and slept or day-dreamt.

He found that the place exactly suited his mood, or rather, had changed his mood in harmony with itself. The oblivion that he desired he now possessed. He found himself completely shut away from those events from which he most wished to escape. It was as if life began anew for him in this quiet house that had not been lived in for so long, but which nevertheless was orderly, clean, and full of beautiful and strange objects, and the isolation soothed his exasperated nerves, and the peculiarity of his lonely situation pleased his fantastical temperament.

It was a perfect summer, the weather itself was sufficient to make a festival. Beyond the garden was the park and beyond the park all his fields and meadows, and beyond again, the sea, a mere glimmer of light in the sunshine.

Mrs. Barlow was always attentive, and the servants knew their work, and he had his own man, Martin, to make him comfortable.

This was a dry, satirical fellow, well trained and shrewd, who remained in Sir William's employ with much fidelity, constant either to his affections or to his interests. He had been not without blame in the affair which had sent his master flying from town, and was glad to be out of the way. When he had followed

Sir William from the city he had brought with him, besides money and clothes, a reassuring letter for his master from a friend.

The affray at the masquerade had been a bad business, no doubt, but it seemed likely to die away without ill consequences, yet it were best that Sir William should keep from town for the summer at least.

The friend had concocted a good story to account for his sudden departure and had so confused the truth that there were many who doubted whether he had been at the masquerade at all. Sir William, on receipt of this letter, had spoken to the servant, whom he held in careless confidence and a kind of negligent, half-contemptuous friendship.

"You are willing to stay with me in this place, Martin? It is to your interests, as I believe, to do so."

The servant repeated in a parrot-like fashion that was not, however, in the least stupid:

"I am quite willing to do so, Sir William. And I believe that it is to your own interest as well as to mine to remain away from town for a while. And if I might give my opinion I should say that Holcot Grange is an ideal place for this retreat."

"It pleases me, for a while," assented the young baronet, "but who knows, Martin, in a moment, one might suddenly tire!"

"It is the novelty that pleases, Sir William," said the servant. "The question is, how long will the novelty endure? It is like a spell which must, sooner or later, wear off."

"Aye, the novelty," laughed Sir William Notley. "No news-sheets, no coffee houses, no riots or carnivals or theatres, no races or sports, no friends or acquaintances, not as much as a barber or a tailor. Novelty indeed, Martin! Come, can you tell me nothing of the place? We have been here several days."

"I know all there is to know, Sir William, and it is very little. Holcot Grange stands far away from the high road, as you found to your cost, I expect, sir, when you were endeavouring to find it, the night you rode from London. The village is very small and the Vicar an old, mild man, sunk in the sloth of age. For the rest it is sheep farming, and the farms very far apart—the village but a handful of cottages. Then there is Mr. Morley at Griffinshaws, who has married a farmer's daughter and lives as if he were a farmer himself."

"But I found him honest," said Sir William; "he gave a good account of his charges. And I thought as I saw him anxiously going over items of even a few pence, 'Consider what a life that man leads for the small amount I pay him.'"

"Philosophy apart, Sir William, he does very well."

"And there is no one else?"

"There is a Miss Julia Roseingrave who lives in the Dower House with her sister, who is idiotic, and her mother, who is like a block of wood from paralysis."

"That is the cool creature who came to see me on the night of my arrival. Do you know, Martin, I have no desire to behold her again, yet I think she is handsome enough."

"And the only woman within miles, Sir William, if your thoughts should turn in that direction."

"They are not like to, Martin. I am now for a chaste and studious life. If I should have an intrigue here it would not be with a creature like Miss Roseingrave—and that's a strange name, too, Martin—but with some milkmaid, some white-handed Hebe, all milk and roses."

"There is none such, I do assure you, sir. The two maids here are coarse, stupid creatures, and only worthy of the swains who have bespoke them."

"Well, let that go, it does not trouble me. And is there no one else with any pretence to breeding besides this Miss Roseingrave?"

"She is very much respected, sir," said Martin, "and lives a very virtuous life. Her devotion to her mother and her sister is very commendable, and I think, Sir William, it would only be a usual courtesy if you were to wait on her. She is, in some manner, your relation."

Sir William was not offended at this advice. He permitted his servant a great freedom.

"Have you seen her, then, Martin?"

"Yes, I took the chance to walk past the Dower House. I went several times before I caught a glimpse of her. I thought her, too, Sir William, a very handsome creature."

"I will not go, I do not know why. As I am here *incognito* it cannot be pronounced a discourtesy. But tell me," added the young baronet, impatiently, "are there no others?"

"There is old Dr. Rowland, sir, who is gently born, and I believe was a scholar at Trinity College once. He lives like a hermit, given up to experiments and speculations."

"As I mean to be," cried the young baronet, "I must make the acquaintance of this fantastic. And who else?"

"No one else at all, sir."

The young man sighed and smiled together, stretched his arms above his head, and went to the window. The peace of the place was incredible. He could scarcely believe in those sunny gardens, in those trees, tossing their high tops in a cloudless blue, in the continuous cooing of the doves and in the profusion of scent of flowers opening their hearts to the last strength of summer.

The room, too,—surely there was a certain spell about this clean apartment where nothing had been moved nor even touched for so many years; where everything had been left exactly in its place, mirrors, in which every face that had ever looked must now be dust, chairs, couches and beds on which none but ghosts could have rested for so long, embroideries, worked by fingers now long withered away, portraits of dead beauties by dead artists, treasures, hoarded long ago, but now neglected, their very meaning incomprehensible. And over all the sunlight, mellow as run honey.

In a closet in one of the upper rooms the young man had found some women's clothes, shoes of wrinkled leather, corsets with rusted steels, and brocades with tarnished tinsel braidings.

"Is there not supposed to be a curse on this house, Martin? I heard Mrs. Barlow, the good housekeeper, speak of it."

"Yes, I have heard that tale, sir," replied Martin, who made it his business to hear all tales wherever he went. "But this is nothing much, only that the property was forfeit during the rebellion and given to a follower of Oliver Cromwell, and when the Restoration came his descendant, a young man, married the heiress of the Royalist family. It was a match of convenience."

"And of mighty convenience, too," laughed Sir William, "since it saved the estates to each."

"But the story goes, as I have heard it from Mrs. Barlow, that they were very unhappy and that he ill-treated her and she died, calling a curse on her descendants, sprung from this union."

"Was she an ancestress of mine?" asked Sir William carelessly. "Perhaps I have inherited this curse. I would it were so, Martin.

There would be a relish and a piquancy about such a fate. I feel, now I have come to this place, that all my days have been very dull."

At this point Mrs. Barlow ventured into the room. She said that a clean old woman who was named Mother Cloke, and against whom indeed no one had ever had any complaints, desired to see Sir William. It would only be to beg some charity of course, but she had been very insistent.

Sir William checked these apologies.

"Do you know anything of this Mother Cloke?" he asked his body-servant.

The man replied:

"She is reputed, Sir William, to be a witch."

Mrs. Barlow was not altogether in favour of Mother Cloke and regarded her coming to the Grange as impertinence, but at the same time she was somewhat in awe of the herb-woman, whom she believed to be something more than her appearance gave warrant for. So she had desired her to wait in the room to the left of the entrance hall, which had once been used for card playing and musical diversions. It was furnished, therefore, with alcoves for tables and in a large press were several musical instruments which had been for long in a sad state of disrepair.

There was only one portrait in the room and that was of a lady in a falling collar, holding in one hand an apple. Both the lady and the fruit seemed to have long ago withered, for it was but a ghostly face and a ghostly apple which gleamed faintly from the faded wood panel.

Mrs. Cloke waited patiently among these splendours so long since unvisited. She had a large basket covered with a white napkin on her arm. When Sir William Notley entered she curtsied very low in a manner that seemed as if she were used to dealing with the gentry, and yet the young baronet had been assured that there were no people of breeding in his neighbourhood.

He liked the look, at once intelligent and meek, of the old woman, and her ready address which was respectful and not servile, pleased him also. She told him that she was a tenant of his, and had lived all her life on the small piece of land for which she paid rent to Mr. Morley of Griffinshaws. Her ancestors, she said, had been tenants of the lords of Holcot Grange for as many years as a man could remember.

"The owners of the Grange were but distantly connected ancestors of mine," said Sir William courteously. "I came into the Grange through my mother's people. She was by birth a Wilbraham."

"You can see all their graves in the chapel if your honour but takes the trouble to look."

"I have not been to the chapel yet, good Mrs. Cloke. It has been long closed up, and I hold it but a dusty business to pry into these dismal places. Yet, for the sake of the dead, through whom I come into this estate, it seems, I will go there, and even, perhaps, set a priest up. And yet if I did who would attend for his ministry, for I shall go away quite soon, and I think there would be no one else to go to this chapel."

"All the farmers, the villagers, the shepherds, would be very glad to go there. The village church is a poor place and this is nearer for most of them."

With that she took the cover off her basket which she had set on one of the walnut tables where cards had been flung down and picked up so often so long ago.

She had brought him, she said, as a gift and a little act of homage from his oldest tenant, some samples of her herbs.

Here in their separate bags were hyssop or mother of time, a decoction of which, made with figs, honey and rue, was good against the cough, and the stiff branches of woody lavender, with the long hoary leaves, which, taken in the morning, fasting, were good for the panting of the heart.

Another bag contained the small shining seeds of fleawort which, pressed into a plaster, were excellent for swelling of the joints. Common pimpernel she had, too, which, though it was but a vulgar weed and growing on wastes, and even barren places, had much virtue in it she declared, for a pottage of this herb would draw out thorns which had been buried in the flesh, or help the dim-sighted when made into a wash for the eyes. From ditches and streams down by the marsh where she lived, and in moist woods, she had plucked the herb twopence, or moneywort, or twopenny grass, which cured ulcers when mixed with resin, wax and turpentine; comfrey she had also, prunel, mouse-ear, cudweed, featherfew, good, she said, for such as are sad and pensive, and eyebright, much commended for the eyes.

While she named and praised these and laid them out severally on the card table, the young baronet listened amused and pleased, for in reaction from what had happened to him in the city, he was gratified by all simple things that served to lull his senses and were different from his usual habits.

She observed him very shrewdly; although she had little experience and had seen few people, she had much natural wisdom.

"Your honour," said she, suddenly coming to an end of her long catalogue, "does not, very like, believe in magic."

He, sighing with a sincere regret, answered as so many others had answered before him:

"I would that I could."

"Some," said she, "give me the name of witch, though I am by no means deserving of that. I have seen strange things, particularly down in Ballote Wood."

"And where's that?" asked he, willing to humour her fantasy.

"That, sir, slopes from the high ground to the marsh, and is near my home; it takes its name from the black horehound, which grows there in quantities and which the rustics call ballote. It has the smell of a citron and the flowers are of a carnation colour, and is a very powerful balm," she added cunningly, "helping much the sudden anguish of love, sir, that affects the heart."

"From which I have never suffered," said Sir William pleasantly. "Yet I must purchase from you some of this balm, good mother. Now tell me some of the mysteries that you have seen in Ballote Wood."

"It would not be safe to do so," she replied quickly. "The young and the gallant ever like curious adventures, and you are both young and gallant, and so I thought to tell you that if you cared, when the moon is full, to walk in Ballote Wood, you might see what would please you."

"So these, then, are not ugly sights?" he asked, teasing, "no apparition of the devil or his attendant fiends?"

"Nay, nothing of that," she said. Then lowering her voice as if they might be overheard, even in the empty room in the empty house, she added: "A nymph or fairy or goddess walks there and bathes in the deep pool underneath the willow trees. I have seen her sometimes when the lunar rays are directly overhead. She shines like a silver spool."

"When can I see this?" asked Sir William, laughing still more, "and what charm must I bring with me to open my eyes? For I believe no ordinary traveller could behold such marvels."

At that Mother Cloke seemed reluctant and would shut up the subject, but he pressed her, swallowing his amusement, though he believed she only feigned the hesitation for art's sake, and to lead him on. No doubt she had a trick up her sleeve, yet her talk had suited his mood. And at last she said in a sudden hurry as if she would be rid of the matter:

"The moon will be full in three days' time, and if you should come to my cottage, sir, I will go with you and show you the place and the person."

"You do not undertake a little matter," said he in hearty mirth. "I am to behold a goddess and at so little cost?"

"Aye, but you must have some charm with you. I will give it you—a bunch of red archangels, tied with a specially woven thread. But leave all that matter to me."

"I will do so very willingly, but see to it, good mother, that you do not dress up some village wench as your goddess. My senses are not so gross but that I should not at once discover the fraud."

"If I do anything so crazy, beat me for an old cheat, your Honour."

VI

When the moon was full, Sir William Notley went down to Ballote Wood and found on the edge of it the cottage of Mother Cloke. This was small, of but two rooms, and close to it were three young oak trees which stood like sentinels on the edge of the battalions of the woods. The place was very lonely and set on the edge of a hill, which appeared rather to be a cliff, as if in the old days the water had come right inland (as it did indeed now, sometimes in the winter or after great storms of rain) along the flat marshes below.

In the daylight these marshes could be seen dotted with white sheep and the little silver lines of small canals, half choked with feathering grasses and bulrushes; in the distance shone the shimmer of the blue sea. In the spring there would be another whiteness, that of blackthorn and hawthorn and daisies, and in the autumn the red and gold of berries.

But none of this could be seen now, only the moon mist that was over everything and the dark shape of the wood.

Sir William Notley knocked at Mother Cloke's door. She opened it in an instant and stood there ready with the bunch of red archangel or dead nettle, which she put into the hand of the young man. As she did so she murmured some words in a *hocus-pocus* language. He took these to be charms and asked her, laughing, if they would protect him against any possible evil in the haunted woods, but her answer surprised him considerably:

"No, it is to protect *me* against *you*."

"To protect yourself against *me*, Goody Cloke." He was curious. "Now what do you fear in me?"

"Something which you do not yet know exists in yourself."

"Evil?" he asked.

"There has been blood on your hands and might be again."

The young man was startled and affronted. The adventure began to take too realistic a turn. His mind was turned back to places where it would not journey willingly.

"Don't frown at me, Sir William," said the old woman, calmly, "I shall neither help nor hinder you on your way. There's others more powerful than I, will do that. I have said I will show you a pretty sight tonight. Think of that, young sir, and of nothing else."

He followed her sullenly along a sloping path which led directly to the woods.

The moonlight was very brilliant. Sir William never remembered to have noticed such a powerful radiance at night before. It cast a blur over everything; the shapes of the trees seemed intangible and a glimpse of marshland below the hill shimmered like a sea of light. The wood was very dark by contrast, and at first he was blinded, and could with difficulty follow the old woman.

"In such a shade as this I should, see nobody if she were to appear."

"Have patience, good Sir William, and follow me. Speak no doubt nor profanity, whether you believe it or no, there is magic abroad."

Then again he wished that it might be so, for he was weary of almost every delight that common joys and ordinary day could provide. So after awhile they came out on to a space where the trees were sparse and in the middle of this was a pool, deep set and overhung by slender boughs of willow saplings, and the frail, tall spikes of loosestrife, their purple blossoms showing like a faint tinge of blood in that silver glow.

Mother Cloke drew the young man behind an oak tree, which stood on the height above this pool, and bade him look down and presently he should see the strange creature, nymph, or goddess, or witch, or she knew not what, who would come and bathe in the pool under the moonlight.

"Goody Cloke," whispered the young man, "if this comes to pass and there be no trick or imposture about it, I will fill up your herb basket with gold pieces."

"And they would be of little use to me," she whispered back, "and I should have to travel very far to be able to spend them. But if your honour can spare, say, half a dozen good bottles of wine from the cellar of Holcot Grange, they would tide me through the winter when I am much troubled with the old cough."

"That you shall have," said he, "the best that can be found. Show me now your goddess."

"Look now, Sir William, and speak no more. Keep your eyes and your mind on the pool."

So the young man looked down, and even without the goddess for whom he waited, the scene was fair enough to snatch him from all bad and evil thoughts.

VII

He had waited but five minutes or so as he judged, but indeed it was difficult to keep time in this place where time seemed to have stopped, when she appeared on the other side of the clearing or open space.

She was naked and held a long twist of black hair in her hand as she came lightly over the ground towards the pool.

At first he did not think of a ruse or trick for she was exceedingly lovely and seemed to him of an immortal cast, and he knew there could be no woman of such a make in these rough and lonely parts; so he stared, his heart panting, thick and frightening, believing he looked on something unearthly.

The woman came through the tall flowers, the nature of which he could not tell by reason of the moonlight dazzle, and so to the edge of the pool where she sat and dipped in her long limbs, and then sank beneath the water and began swimming across so that only her head and the black hair floating like a weed, showed.

And then the young man recovered his senses.

He said: "It is a mortal woman," and prepared to run down the bank. But the herb woman held him back with a surprising strength.

"If you stir or say a word, she will vanish."

And so, because he still, against his will, feared some magic, the young man stayed his impetuous movement and stared down through the leafage on to the pool where her face floated like a water lily and her hair like a dark leaf; and looking down into that face, which remained still for a moment on the surface of the water with closed eyes and slightly parted lips and all the light of the moon turning the flesh to an unearthly look of silver, he knew himself lost, and he tried to turn and escape away through the haunted darkness of Ballote Wood, but the old beldame clung to him and impeded him and bade him watch, and still watch, so he stared again down to the pool.

The woman stirred in the limpid waters; her shoulders, her bosom, her arms and hands rose from out the pool. She opened her eyes and looked up at him. Her wet hair clung, a dark tracery, on the whiteness of her body.

She stared up at the oak tree behind which he hid, as if she saw him, yet he thought that it was impossible that she could do so.

"It is an earthly woman," he repeated, "but who?"

"Follow her and see," said Mother Cloke, stretching up to his ear.

The bather swam across the pool again, and bending the tall flowers that grew on the bank, stepped out into the sheer moonlight which clothed her from head to foot as modestly as a veil. He saw her blurred by this radiance; he could observe only that she was tall and curved and very slender and surely unearthly after all...

He watched her wring out the long black hair and saw how the drops sparkled like diamonds as they fell from her hands to nothingness about her feet.

She crossed the open space of blossoming, gleaming weeds, and entered the grove of young trees the other side, and he, watching her, saw her pick up some garment and put it about her shoulders.

He looked round for Mother Cloke, but the herb woman had gone and he made little matter of that. The adventure that was to have been but a phantasy or a delusion had proved real enough.

Agile and resolute he lowered himself down the bank and he also, skirting the pool, crossed the clearing. As he neared the grove where the woman robed herself, she moved away, but not so far as to be lost among the trees, and not so rapidly but that he could follow her. And follow her he did, keeping a few paces behind until they had left the wood and come out into the park. He could see her very clearly. It was a night of sullen warmth and he observed that her hair was already dry and strands blowing loose over the light cloak or robe that she wore.

He followed her to a grove of chestnut trees and directly to the honeysuckle porch of the Dower House and there she turned and faced him as if she had known all along that he was behind her, and yet he had flattered himself that he had been very discreet, hiding continually behind the trees and in shrubs, and walking very softly.

When she paused in the porch he was still some paces away, half behind one of the chestnut trees, but she beckoned with her hand, which was like a lily waving in the wind, and he came forward and stood at the gate of her little garden which was packed with carnations that gave forth a strong night perfume.

"I am Julia Roseingrave," she said, "what do you want with me?"

He did not answer for he did not know, and he felt, too, ashamed of himself, and remorseful that he had been taken in by the old woman's trick, if trick it were and not some strange chance, and so he stood mute, which was not his usual way with women.

"Oh, you are but a dullard," said Julia Roseingrave, coolly, "and I liked Ballote Wood better before you came prying there."

At that she went into the darkness of the Dower House and shut the door in his face.

VIII

Sir William Notley was enchanted, as the two women had intended that he should be. Nothing now would please him but the possession of Julia Roseingrave. Though she might appear to the casual eye but an ordinary woman in her clothes, he knew that in herself she was as beautiful as a lily spike, as a branch of silver bells. He knew, too, that she was strange and cold and had lived all her life apart from the world.

He liked to think that she were a witch or a fairy or possibly a goddess, and that Mother Cloke, who had beguiled him into the woods, was her handmaiden or attendant. Perhaps they were evil, both of them, but for that he cared nothing. The herb woman had said that he was evil, too. He was even pleased by the thought that she lived alone in the park in the Dower House with those two stricken creatures. He felt that strange exaltation which was always his, when he fell in or out of love.

He did not immediately endeavour to see her, but for two days after he had beheld her bathing in the pool in Ballote Wood, he stayed in the house or went abroad but in the garden at sunset, when the doves were homing and all the flowers giving out their evening scent.

He took out the old instruments from the press in the room where he had first met the herb woman, and repaired them, for he had great skill in music. He wrested the keys aright, and tuned them and restrung the stringed instruments, he tenderly oiled and polished the delicate woods. Some were cracked and beyond repair, but others only needed careful handling which he gave them, to emit again their sweet, mournful melodies.

The harpsichord was easily put aright, for Mrs. Barlow had kept it oiled and cleaned. He had flowers in large glass cups brought into this room and the windows set open so that the sun came in, and he asked Mrs. Barlow when she was doing this work for him, who was the original of the portrait—the pale lady with the withered apple?

She replied that it was the Lady Dorcas, who had set the curse on the Grange and her descendants—that was one reason, said Mrs. Barlow, why it had been so long uninhabited. As long as a man had another house he did not care to live in Holcot Grange.

Sir William laughed.

"I have seldom seen a pleasanter place nor one where a man might be more readily at peace."

Mrs. Barlow looked at him with a certain apprehension. She thought him very handsome yet she was not altogether attracted by him, the expression was too wilful and imperious, and the splendour of his youth was something tarnished—good Mrs. Barlow did not know by what. She dreaded him and did not like his residence at the Grange, she could not get over the impression she had received the night of his arrival, when she thought she had admitted the Devil into the old house, yet his manners to her were always civil and even courteous and he was lavish with his money to all the servants. Mrs. Barlow did not like Martin either. The man was taciturn and would say nothing of what had happened to his master or to himself in London.

While Sir William Notley dallied with the after-taste of his nocturnal adventure in Ballote Wood, the weather changed. The brilliant sunshine disappeared, but not behind any cloud; it was, rather, obscured by a subtle mist, light, yet not to be penetrated, as if mysteries were to be performed in Heaven, which must be veiled from the earth. This withdrawal of the light was not without a certain menace, but the young man found it much to his taste. While Mrs. Barlow talked with an odd apprehension of a coming storm, he noted curiously the changes that this mist gave to the house, the gardens, and the landscape, still to him so unfamiliar.

The gardens greatly interested him; the sombre man who worked there had done his duty skilfully, and it was that season in the year, the height of summer turning into autumn, that the strangest and most gorgeous flowers were in bloom. The young man admired the *Rosa Ultramarina* or Outlandish Rose, with the bright purple, double blossoms rising high above all the more lowly plants and the Indian Sun, heavy with seeds, hanging languidly and not knowing to which part of the heavens to turn since the sun was hid.

He noted the helmet-shaped, blue flowers of the Monkshood, the delicate tints of the Dovesfeet, and when he saw the small red grapes of the woodbine or honeysuckle, he thought of Julia Roseingrave standing under the porch of the Dower House.

At night the mist was denser than it had been in the day; moist exhalations rose from the low, fenny ground beyond the woods and the park, and these divided into the likeness of large, strange shapes that floated up and away into the dim upper radiance. Mrs. Barlow entertained an intense conviction that it was dangerous to go out at night and to breathe in deeply the marsh mist.

He took no heed of her warning, but walked abroad in the quadrangle right up to the iron gates that had been opened for the first time in so many years, to admit him in his devil's disguise.

And then in the garden to the *quidnuncs* where the narrow box hedges were kept carefully clipped, and in the centre was a great globe of metal tarnished by damp.

The young man had left lights in an upper room of the Grange and the windows open, for he liked to look back and see the place thus illuminated as if somebody were waiting to receive and welcome him on his return. The Grange was silent in the daytime, but even more profound was the silence of the night, for there were not the homely noises of the servants going to and fro in their quarters, nor the bark of a dog, nor the low of a sheep or cow to be heard, nor the cooing of the doves. All living creatures were mute.

Sir William recognised something unhealthy and evil in the marsh mist; the air was heavy and close. When he looked back at the Grange he saw that not one of his lights had stirred, because no breath of wind floated through the open windows. There was a little pavilion at the far end of the garden close to a small pond or, rather, a great stone basin of water, in the centre of which had once been a fountain, but the machinery had been neglected and the waters no longer played from the pipes concealed in the moss-greened dolphins in the centre of the pond. There were dark weeds and white lilies on the water and through the mist Sir William could see them and they reminded him, though he needed no such aid to his remembrance for her face was constantly before him, of the creature whom he had seen bathing in the depths of Ballote Wood, her dark hair like the pond weeds, and face and shoulders and bosom white as the lilies.

He tried to recall the expression of her eyes when she had looked up at him, neither trustful nor beckoning, nor suspicious, but a look of blank acceptance as if she drew all his soul into hers as a matter of course, as a casual gift. He wondered if she had been sleep walking on that night, or if it were her ghost that he had seen.

He knew the old tale—that the ghosts of those about to die in the ensuing year wandered round the churchyard near the spot where they were likely to lie.

Had he then disturbed Julia Roseingrave while she had been returning from a visit to her future tomb?

The *miasmas* from the marsh had invaded the painted pavilion, which was damp from being long shut away and had no furniture beyond a couch of gilded wood very tarnished.

The young man stood at the door of this pavilion and looked out across the lily pond at the stone figure of the great fish, at the poisonous mists which rose and slowly dispersed in the upper moonlit air. Above, was a curious silver gloom, unreal and fascinating; his own swarthy brow, lowering glance, and dark clothes were not ill-fitted to the scene, nor was his mood.

He thought of his past life and all the deeds he had done as shut away in a book... he endeavoured by this symbol to express his complete severance from his former life, shut away in a book and clasped, locked, and sealed.

He strained his ears against the silence, half expecting a voice of warning or of menace or of invitation, and it seemed to him that he was lifted up and away from the earth, but not towards any heaven.

He had hitherto ridden towards his destiny with a loose rein, careless as to the consequences of his pleasures, his wanton sins, of temptations unresisted, indifferent as to the morrow, and contemptuous of Hell.

Now, with his past shut so resolutely behind him, he felt as if he had his fate in grip, and could and would deliberately choose his own path, and in that moment he felt disdainful both of good and evil, as if he held fiends and archangels helpless in the palm of his hand. He remained near the pavilion until the dawn.

With the first pallor of eastern light a little breeze arose and set the lilies rocking in the pond, and fluttered those few candles in the upper rooms of the Grange that had not yet burnt out.

The marsh mist divided and hung for a second or so in the likeness of ghostly, hooded, shrouded figures, then dispersed, and the air was pure.

Sir William walked back to the house.

The flowers looked strange in that first light, many of them were yet folded, their petals closed over their hearts, all were pearled by the moisture of the night. They were entangled in a great luxuriancy, and the leaves of many had begun to decay and turn yellow.

IX

Sir William went to the dower house and looked at it earnestly before he knocked for admission.

The garden, unlike the garden of the Grange, was small, modest, and homely. There were no weeds nor any faded flowers. Even the most prodigal sweets of the summer were pruned and trained. And the front of the small brick house had an innocent, care-free look. Clean white curtains were at the windows, the panes of glass shone brightly, being newly rubbed, and the honeysuckle over the porch had been tied back with a careful hand.

The young man thought that all this air of orderly decorum was a mere deception or part of a snare.

He knocked at the door. He had been so sure that she would open to him that the look on his face was for her and for her only. He was therefore amazed when a man stood before him holding the doorknob in his hand and greeting him with a ready courtesy.

"You are Sir William Notley? Miss Roseingrave saw you from the window and asked me to admit you at once."

"And who, sir, are you?" asked the young baronet, sullenly. He felt the flavour of the afternoon spoiled by the intrusion of the personality of this stranger.

"I am Dr. Rowland, and I ride over sometimes to attend to Mrs. Roseingrave. Not that anything can be done for her," he added confidentially, lowering his voice as the two stood together in the narrow passage, "but I believe that my occasional presence is some comfort to Miss Julia."

Sir William eyed the physician with disdain.

He was a man past middle age with an air of great vitality and energy. The cut of his murrey-coloured suit was long out of date, but he was neat and orderly in his attire. His limbs were well made and well knit and there was a cast of nobility in his haggard face round which the pale hair, half blond, half grey, curled like a mane.

He courteously stood aside while Sir William preceded him to a little parlour, overstocked with small, bright, shining objects where Julia Roseingrave sat behind a tea service of pale blue china.

She wore a linen gown, that had been many times washed and mended, fastened with scoured, ironed green ribbon. The long swathes of her dark hair were fastened by iron pins and there was nothing about her that was not faded and common.

Sir William thought that this decorous poverty was like the respectable exterior of the house, part of the disguise and the snare.

Dr. Rowland took his leave almost immediately; he displayed neither curiosity nor deference towards Sir William, only a rather abstracted courtesy, and when he had left the house the young man remarked:

"You are strange people here, you live in an isolation where nothing seems to have ever happened, yet when the unusual occurs you do not marvel at it."

"That is Dr. Rowland," said Miss Roseingrave, replying obliquely to this comment. "He lives a long way from here and I do not often see him. I cannot suppose that a man like that would ever be greatly surprised at anything. His studies are very abstruse and take him into other worlds."

"But you," he asked directly, "you have no such consolation in your solitude. I hear from Mrs. Barlow, who is a good gossip, that your mother and your sister are both ill. You must, then, have very little company."

"Very little human company," she replied.

"Then you, also, Miss Roseingrave, know something of those other worlds with which Dr. Rowland is familiar?"

She poured out the steaming tea into the shallow blue cups and offered him one. The sun had begun to penetrate very faintly the mist, so that a dim pattern of light fell through the waving boughs of the woodbine into the small room.

"If I were to tell you of my life here and the company I have, and what goes on on the marsh and in the woods, aye, and even in the open pastures, you would no more believe it than I should be able to credit you, were you to tell me what your life was in the city."

"I shall never tell you that," he countered, "for I wish to forget it myself."

She directly challenged that.

"Why? Everything that has ever happened to me I wish to remember."

Sir William smiled unpleasantly, and gulped his tea. It was the first time that he ever recalled having tasted that beverage, for he had always avoided the company of gentlewomen.

"You do not wish to tell me," said Julia Roseingrave, coolly. "Well, no doubt, you were concerned in something frightful or you never would have come to Holcot Grange. And, of course, you will not stay, as soon as you realise that you are out of danger."

It seemed to the young man, sitting there holding the blue cup in his hands, that there was another voice behind hers which rose shrill and high like an echo, and said: "Fly, you are in more danger now than you ever were in your life." So intense was this impression that he glanced round the room to see if, small as the apartment was, there might not be somebody concealed behind one of the pieces of furniture, who had thus mocked her and him. But they were alone together.

She marked his glance and asked:

"What are you considering? You are not at all open with me, Sir William. You were very short when I first saw you on the night of your arrival at the Grange. It was strange, no doubt, for me to come into your chamber like that, but remember that poor Mrs. Barlow came running up through the night and told me that she had admitted the Devil."

"You were courageous," he mocked, "seeing that you do not believe in the Devil or maybe are his ally."

"And you are blunt," she replied indifferently. "I have never met a fine gentleman before. I had thought you would have been more courteous. Why have you paid me the honour of this visit?—I do not think we shall greatly amuse each other."

"Oh, Miss Roseingrave," he exclaimed impatiently and rising as he spoke, "will you not come with me into the woods? It is so close and confined here."

"I may not leave my mother and sister," she answered. "At present my mother sleeps, my sister plays with her white rabbits, but at any moment my mother may wake and Phœbe may begin to cry."

Sir William walked up and down the room, which his great height and lordly presence made appear as cabined and as contemptible as a cage.

"The herb woman whom they call Goody Cloke, she is your friend, is she not?"

"She is an acquaintance of mine, Sir William, she works for me. She is the only person whom I can find who is willing to drudge for my mother and sister. This is not accounted a cheerful house and I can afford to pay very little."

He gave her a sidelong look where she sat sipping her tea primly and thought of all his life had been, as a schoolboy, as a scholar at Oxford, as a young man travelling in Italy and France, of the people whom he had met and the adventures he had had, and the large sums of money he had spent and thrown away, and all the while Julia Roseingrave had been sitting in the Dower House, drinking tea, going about her small duties, and, with the aid of the herb woman, attending a paralysed mother and an imbecile sister, and throughout all there had been ahead of him and of her, the day when they were bound to meet. He said:

"I walked in Ballote Wood the other night and saw a nymph bathing."

"You may, sir," said she, "see many worse, and many better things in Ballote Wood."

"If I go there again shall I see her again?" he challenged; and her eyes that had that smouldering light in them, like a flame reflected in a tablet of polished jet, were full on him as she answered:

"I can assure you that you will not. No one who pries in Ballote Wood sees the same thing twice."

"Stop this fencing or play of words," said he. "Could not you love me a little?"

Miss Roseingrave set down her tea-cup and put her smooth hand to her smooth hair that was slipping slightly from the iron pins.

"I could love no man a little," she answered; "I have a scorn for love measured out, aye, or passion, by the thimbleful."

"What do you know," he asked, half-angrily, "of either love or passion?"

"Enough, Sir William, to fill all my days and nights with dreams," she said, but more with uneasiness than contempt. "You are here for a space," she smiled, "hiding, as I think, at odds with your usual fortunes, concealed from the handlings of mischance. And you wish for a pleasant interlude, a play of shadows—love-in-idleness. Well, I shall not be your partner."

"Why?" he demanded, pausing full in front of her.

The sun had brightened again and the room was full of yellow light, only broken by the waving shadows of the woodbine—torn flowers, red tendrils, and scarlet berries blown sideways from the porch.

"Perhaps you do not please me," she said coldly, and at that he raged, for no woman had ever scorned him before, but all, out of liking or interest or fear, had flattered him.

"You think to lead me on by tricks," he stormed sullenly. "You think to set on yourself a higher value than you have."

Miss Julia Roseingrave got to her feet with one graceful movement and set down her blue tea-cup.

"Have you ever met a proud woman before?" she asked lazily. "Go, and I shall not follow. Turn away, and I shall not beckon you back."

He was forced to assume a humility that he did not feel.

"Come, pretty one, there is a full summer's month before us and I am weary of common delights, and you, I think, have never known them—"

"Youth goes so fast, is that your common conclusion?" she jeeringly interrupted. "I shall not care when I am old. Youth or age is the same to me."

"But not to me," he answered, suddenly serious. "I hope to die as soon as I lose the first *iota* of my strength and power." Then he fell a-coaxing. "Come, play with me a little, pretty one. Take me on to the marsh and show me the strange people that live there. Smugglers are there not, and eel-catchers in their huts and old wise women and shepherds who see nothing but their sheep all the year long? Come up with me to the Grange. There are many secrets in that house and I have discovered none of them yet. Be my partner in that adventure. We will have quests through all those rooms that have been so long since closed."

"And raise the ghosts?" she queried. "They say, you know, that the place is cursed."

"Maybe. How should that concern us? If we be cursed I doubt if we can avoid our fate. Come up to the Grange, I need an audience for my music. I have put into order some old instruments I found there."

"I shall not care for your London airs," she replied. "I, too, am a musician. I have here, in the next room, a harp and a spinet on which I play very fairly."

"No doubt you have all the arts and all the graces," he mocked. "It is a strange thing to me that you have been shut away here so long. I swear that you have a secret and that I shall surprise it."

A steady wailing broke the afternoon silence. He had forgotten the imbecile girl and was startled. The sound seemed like the cry of one in mortal distress.

"It is my sister Phœbe," said Miss Roseingrave, with what seemed a malicious pleasure. "I told you she would not be long quiet."

The door opened and the idiot girl entered. She was thin, and dark, and pale, and had a certain likeness to her sister. Her hair straggled from under a white mob cap, she wore an untidy cotton gown and held in her arms a dead white rabbit. Her eyes were vacant, her lips blubbered as she cried and caressed the limp shape of the little animal.

"See, she has strangled it," said Miss Julia, "that is how her play always ends. It is the same with the doves and the kittens. You had best go, Sir William. You see we are not a pleasant household."

But he was not a man to be shocked by cruelty, nor by any strange nor displeasing sight.

He said: "Send Goody Cloke up to look after the poor, deranged creature and come abroad with me."

She replied: "It is not duty but lack of interest in your company that bids me stay."

He snatched at his gloves and his hat, and left the Dower House.

He did not take the path that led under the chestnut trees through the park towards the Grange, but passed on beyond into loneliness.

He skirted a meadow where the moon-daisies grew in the second haysel, where the berries of the arum or cuckoo pint ripened underneath the tangle of the rough bindweed. The stagnant wet beneath the hedges was full of the leaves of the water caltrops.

By these open places he made his way to Ballote Wood. The trees were mostly ash and now the mist had cleared, every leaf on every bough showed clear and vivid in the westering light. It was silent but not absolutely still. Small wild things could be heard running and almost breathing through the shrubs and herbage. After sundry mistakings of his way, for there were no paths in the wood, Sir William reached the pool where he had seen Julia Roseingrave or her wraith bathing. Thrusting aside the sorrel and loosestrife that bordered the sloping side, and lifting the sprays of willow, he looked down into the lilied pool, almost hoping again to behold that white face, that drifting wreath of black hair, but all he saw was the reflection of his own scowling brow and petulant pouting lips and dark town clothes that were an affront to the light and freedom of the day and the careless peace of the place.

X

Dr. Rowland worked day and night at his golden secrets. He was more used to the stars than to the earth, more at home in space than on solid ground.

He lived in an oasthouse that had been used for the drying of hops in the old days, but it was long since hops had been grown in this part of the country. The little furnace was kept alight by Dr. Rowland for other purposes than that of making savouring for beer. There was a two-roomed cottage attached to the oasthouse, and there, when he was not deep in his experiments, he lived. There was a stable, too, and one sound horse in it, and a boy who came from a farm two miles off to look after the beast, and sometimes to draw water and chop wood for Dr. Rowland.

But for the most the learned man was his own servant. He sometimes so far neglected himself that for days together he would go without any food beyond a dry crust he might find in the closet, or a handful of wild fruit that he might gather in his wanderings, or the offerings of pies and preserves that he sometimes found on his doorstep, left by the grateful farm people whose sicknesses he tended without fee or reward.

The oasthouse was situated about five miles from Holcot Grange and low down on the marsh only a pace or two away from where the ground was below the sea level and commonly flooded. After rare heavy rains the oasthouse would be flooded also, and Dr. Rowland would have to move to the friendly shelter of some distant farm until the waters had subsided.

On these occasions he would bring with him, in great packs on the horse, all his precious instruments and retorts and limbecks, his cases of herbs, his packages of powders.

Dr. Rowland and his occupations did not cause the wonder on the marsh that they would have caused in the city. Everyone accepted him as a character both natural and admirable. They were all a little afraid of him, but it was a pleasurable kind of fear, such as a man might feel for an archangel. They did not question his learning nor mock at his wisdom; they believed that it was as right as it was wonderful that he should strive after the secrets of nature and of the skies. They believed that he endeavoured to discover the secret of making gold; yet why should Dr. Rowland devote so much labour and time to discovering how to manufacture yellow metal that would have been but dross to him? All his needs were satisfied and he had no hankering after any earthly ambition. Though he was not much more than middle-aged he had discovered greater wonders than he had ever hoped to achieve in a lifetime, and stumbled upon many a discovery that amazed himself.

His life, although he lived in such isolation, was very rich and varied and full of excitement. The only woman who had ever been inside his laboratory was Julia Roseingrave, and she came secretly after twilight.

XI

The moon had waned and the night was clear and dark save for the clustering brilliance of the stars which made a radiance more likely to confuse than to illuminate.

Sir William Notley felt himself utterly plucked away from his old life, he knew the even freedom of a man whose days have always been stainless. He had no burden of remembered sins. He felt at ease with his own soul, and in harmony with all about him.

When his city acquaintances sent him letters, which they did cautiously and severally, he burnt them without reading them. He wrote to no one. The care of the estate remained in the hands of Mr. Morley of Griffinshaws, and the master of Holcot Grange and of so many other houses and estates lived on his own property as if he were a stranger and a guest there. His state became a very ecstasy of dreams and languid inaction. He made no effort to pursue Julia Roseingrave, it was enough for him to know that she was there in the Dower House with the woodbine ripening on the porch, behind the chestnut trees in the park.

He rejoiced in the fair weather, in the ineffable stillness of the long summer afternoons which held, surely, in their remote golden hours an echo of eternity. He listened with drowsy content to the song of the reapers and came to take it as part of the harvest (there was but a field or so of it on the estate); he watched the reaping-hooks laying low the bearded grain and the corn lilies and the corn roses that grew between the brittle yellow stalks.

Behind the song of the reapers which he felt to be melancholy and uncouth he seemed often to hear that other high voice, which he believed he had first caught the accent of in Julia Roseingrave's neat parlour—an unearthly voice which said: "You are in more peril than you have ever been before."

This warning, even though he believed it true, mattered little to him. If he were foreshadowed by his own fate, he cared nothing. He felt himself to be in possession of some persuasive and all-pervading truth which made all the incidents of human life unimportant, reconciled good and evil, and took the horror from crime, and the abnegation from duty, and blended both in one perpetual delight.

He was in that mood when the conflicting forces that divide Creation seemed united in his heart. There had been a time, and that not so long ago, though it seemed so far away, when he had been in the thick of that conflict. Now he was apart from it, and, as-it seemed, for ever. A voluptuous sensation of acquiescence in things as they were, lulled his senses and his spirits. He ate very sparingly and he slept long, and his health became finer than it had been since he was a youth, and he had up some of the rose-coloured wine from the cellars, laid down and sealed by a dead hand so many years ago.

And in the evening he would sit with the windows open and watch the stars glittering like falling jewels among the high elm trees, and raise his glass and drink to Julia Roseingrave.

It was his decision that she should come to him; he would make no further step in the wooing of her. His waiting did not gall him, he felt no trepidation as to the result. One sunny morn, or one starlit eve, or one dense midnight she would come up to the Grange and be his entirely.

But Julia Roseingrave made no sign. The new moon waxed large again in the sky and became strong enough to fade the starlight, and still she did not come. He saw nothing of Mother Cloke the herb woman nor of Dr. Rowland. The gardens became full of seed pods and fruit and withering leaves and drying blossoms.

The stubble field from which the harvest had been carted away looked bleached white in the sunlight. The last swallows were flying very low.

For a long while it had not rained and the vegetation was dried and brittle.

Sir William went several times to the lily pond in Ballote Wood and the water there was drying up and the lilies fading. His unrestrained and libertine fancy kept him inactive. He never turned his steps towards the Dower House beyond the chestnut trees in the park.

One night, after a day of heavy dreams, he saw the thunder-clouds coming up behind the elm trees, packs of vapour, advancing and mingling with the natural dark. He felt at once enervated and excited by the menace of the approaching storm; several birds flew home in the murky twilight, their crying sounded like shrieks of terror. Mrs. Barlow wanted to set lights in every room; she was afraid of thunderstorms, she could remember some terrible tempests coming up from the sea and striking the marsh and the woods, blasting many trees, and killing sheep and even human beings.

But Sir William dismissed her. He found a sensuous charm in this majestic disturbance of the elements. He sat at his open window and cast a clear and penetrating glance into the dark turmoil of the heavens. He thought that perhaps she would come tonight; he believed that his withdrawal was wearing down her lofty and contemptuous spirit, and soon she must surrender, and he waited, drowsy and eager, for her to come fearlessly through the dark and the storm. With his own hand he even set a supper on the heavy waxed and shining oak table: fruit, and wine, and sweet cakes.

Something, his conscience, his heart, or that high voice he had heard singing above the reaper's song, warned him that her coming might be little conducive to his future peace or welfare, but he recklessly continued in a delicious moment of expectation.

There was an intense stillness as if every living thing down to the smallest of weeds in the crevice of the walls were motionless, and as if every breathing thing down to the most timid mouse in the wainscot held its breath.

Then the storm broke directly above the Grange.

Sir William felt peace, satisfaction, and repose as he stood beneath this opulent display of celestial fury. He saw the heavenly fires flash beyond the window, showing in a second's greenish brilliancy the outline of the elm trees, the garden, the vases of withered flowers on the terrace. Or, if he turned to another window, showing the bare quadrangle and the great iron gates through which he had ridden in the tawdry, red rags with which so gaily he had adorned himself as a mock devil.

She could not, of course, bold and fearless as she was, come through the full fury of the tempest, but he looked for her immediately afterwards.

The storm was short, the thunder rolled and muttered away towards the West and seemed to draw the oppressive heat with it. The lightning diminished to mere sparkles on the dim horizon far beyond the marsh. The stars showed behind the light, hurrying vapour; the moon had already set, and silence and a gentle breeze came like a benison on the land.

Sir William set the silver lamp in the window. It was to guide her, for he was still sure that she would come. He glanced at the table to see that all was set fairly; he held up a crystal flagon of wine so that the light of the lamp was reflected in the heart of it—rosy gold it was, old and perfumed. He turned about the peaches that had ripened on the southern red brick walk of the fruit garden. He had collected some small early pale-yellow apples, wall pears and plums with the bloom unimpaired, taken from the muslin bags which protected them from wasp and fly.

He took off his dark coat and fetched from the press one of a ruby-coloured velvet, with long skirt and wide cuffs that he had made the fashion in the city through the mere wearing of it at Court. He looked round for a mirror, but there was none in the room—and still she did not come.

He went down to the door and set it wide and looked across the quadrangle. Surely she would arrive through the iron gates. That would please her, he had eased and left them ajar on purpose, she had but to touch the cold metal and it would yield. The night was no longer very dark, the glimmer of the stars was sufficient and the way was very familiar to her, but still she did not come.

And when the dawn, with unusual magnificence, suddenly coloured the East with saffron he knew that she would not come, and for the first time since his arrival at Holcot Grange he felt a definite disappointment, a definite uneasiness.

XII

With the full daylight Sir William rode over to Dr. Rowland's strange dwelling, which he had some difficulty in finding; he had indeed to pause several times to ask his direction, once from a woman standing scouring a bowl at the door of a solitary cottage, and once from a shepherd, sitting on a knoll covered with wild thyme, watching his sheep.

It was a very fair, pure day, and there were larks singing in the upper air, and as Sir William rode across the fields and the hedgerows and out on the open ground that skirted the lower marsh he could discern in the distance, the shimmer of the blue sea. But for all that he no longer felt the ease and harmony which had been his for the last few days. That state of expectancy had been, indeed, too perfect to last. He was even touched by a certain fear and frequently looked behind him as he rode, though all around him was so clear and open that no one could have followed him nor lurked at his side, for there was nowhere for anyone to hide.

When he reached the oasthouse Dr. Rowland himself came at once to the door and greeted him with the same emphatic courtesy he had used when he had met him at the Dower House.

Without any explanation of or excuse for his lack of service, Dr. Rowland himself took Sir William's horse to the small stable, and then returned and conducted him to the room underneath the laboratory, which was reached by a ladder stairway and from which came faint fumes of chemicals.

Dr. Rowland wore an ancient coat, stained and scorched from his various experiments. His hands in places were dyed with bluish patches, an overworn ribbon caught back his mane-like hair, and large spectacles disguised his piercing eyes.

Courteously he bade the young man be seated. Without any sign of haste or curiosity he waited for him to disclose his business, and Sir William came to this without any preamble.

"I want to know," he asked, "what you can tell me of Miss Julia Roseingrave?"

Dr. Rowland answered at what appeared a tangent.

"Ah, of course, you are the young baronet, are you not? You own the whole estate and others beside. Those three creatures live on your charity."

Sir William was angered at this, which was spoken in a tone of contempt, for he had never been ungenerous in these matters.

"I do not name it charity," he answered dryly. "Had they the whole Grange and all the estates for their pleasure, it had made little difference to me. I am not as rich as I was, but I have still sufficient not to miss the gift of Holcot Grange."

"Ah, you boast, as the young and the rich and the well-favoured always do," smiled Dr. Rowland. "No doubt it does not show much kindness in you to spare a house you do not want. I have thought before that you might have made some little provision beyond the Dower House for their poverty is very keen."

"I did not even know of their existence and now I know very little about them."

"What does their history really matter?" interrupted Dr. Rowland, pointing his finger in the direction of the young man's heart.

"Nothing indeed, to me, nothing, but—Madam Julia? You seem to be her only friend. What do you know of her?"

"The same as you know, Sir William, that she lives in that house in the middle of your park and tends her mother and her sister, and goes to church when she can be spared. She is very neat in her ways and she is dutiful in her behaviour."

"I think all that," said Sir William, lowering his voice, "which I have remarked to be a delusion or even a snare. I do not consider this woman to be what she seems."

"Why?" asked the Doctor coolly. He took off his glasses and wiped them on his sleeve, his eyes seemed to be heavy, bloodshot and weary.

"I think of my own life and I think of hers," said the young man earnestly. "I remember how I have lived all my days. We are much of an age, and she, I would swear, is no saint cut in marble on a tombstone, or in stone above a church door. She is flesh and blood. She has lived alone like that, without company, without love, without excitement? What is her secret? What is her charm?"

"You must find that out for yourself," replied the doctor, "for indeed I do not know it."

"I thought," confessed Sir William sullenly, "that she would find some diversion in my company." He hesitated, he seemed half likely to tell his adventure in Ballote Wood, but he held his tongue about this, partly because he thought that he played a ridiculous part in the tale, partly because there was something about it he wished to keep as his own secret.

He then related how he had waited day after day for Miss Roseingrave to come to the Grange and how he had expected her after the storm. Dr. Rowland laughed in a way that the young man found very little flattering.

"If you want her you must go after her. She is not a woman to come to a whistle. Nay, I do not think you would be able, were you to search for ten years, to find a spell strong enough to lure Julia Roseingrave to you."

The young man caught at the word "spell."

"Do you know any charms?" he asked, half mocking, half earnest. "Is there some potion that I could bribe Goody Cloke to put into that pale tea she drinks, that would make her come to me when I beckon? Any incantation I can mutter the next time the moon is full to make her walk through Ballote Wood or a meeting-place I should appoint?"

"I know of none," said Dr. Rowland. He looked at him straightly with his exhausted yet brilliant eyes, "and, Sir William, you disturb me. I have my crucible on the furnace above. I am now, as always, on the verge of some strange, some golden secret."

"Alchemy?" asked the young man, not without interest; he had, in his time, made his experiments.

"Hermetic Philosophy," corrected Dr. Rowland.

"And what have you discovered, my learned philosopher?"

"Enough to keep my lips sealed, Sir William."

"I would pay you very well for some of this secret knowledge of yours."

"There is nothing you could give me, for I have all that I want."

"You have found then the secret of making gold?"

"I have more gold than suffices my needs," parried Doctor Rowland.

"Then you might have helped those three women with whose poverty you have reproached me."

"Perhaps I have done so," said the Doctor gravely. "How do you know that they had not starved were it not for my help?"

"As poor as that," said Sir William, not without a malicious pleasure, "then surely I have been too cautious, too timid. She can be bribed, if you may not be."

"How could you bribe her?" asked Dr. Rowland cautiously, staring at the blue stains on his hands.

"I should think—with anything! Surely she would be pleased enough to leave the woods, the park. Why, she has never been more than a few miles from where she lives since she came here twenty years ago."

"You would no more move her than you would the foxgloves," said Dr. Rowland. "They die when they are transplanted, you know."

"Has she no ambitions, no desires?" asked the young baronet impatiently. "Come, you must know her heart if anyone does. Does she never sicken or weary of that wretched idiot, that paralysed woman, for company? Does she never want gay gowns nor jewels nor a festival nor a lover?"

"Go and ask her that yourself," answered Dr. Rowland indifferently.

"Aye, and so I will. But I have ridden here for your judgment, for your opinion."

"Why should I give it you, Sir William?"

"Oh, I grant that you are not interested in me, nor my fortunes, but, say, for the sake of Miss Julia Roseingrave, so that I may know how to approach her without offence."

Dr. Rowland had gone to the ladder which led to his laboratory above. He paused there with one hand on the wooden rungs and looked back over his powerful shoulder as he answered:

"I would say that her dreams suffice her. That it were better for you and for her if you left her with those same dreams."

Sir William was disappointed and angered. He left the old house and fetched his horse and rode back to Holcot Grange, not to the mansion, but straight through the park and under the chestnut trees to the Dower House. He fastened loosely the bridle to one of the lower boughs and entered the little garden, still stocked with pinks. The flowers seemed to last longer here than in any other place he had noticed near by, he thought as he passed under the fruiting bindweed and knocked on the porch.

It was she who opened to him, and immediately, as if she had been waiting for him behind the door.

She had on a thin dress of fine old silk, cowslip coloured and furbished, of a design of black violets on the sleeves and at the bosom. Her black hair was fastened with silver bodkins, she appeared to have prepared herself carefully for some extraordinary occasion. He came swiftly across the threshold and asked her why she had kept him waiting so long.

"For what?" asked she, and closed the door on him.

They stood close together in the narrow passage. Phœbe, from an upper room, was singing, plaintively, it was not a disagreeable nor a disturbing sound for a lovesick man; he took her by the arms.

"You were expecting me?" she asked, without fear, but not, he thought, without a certain edge of triumph to her voice, and he sacrificed his pride.

"Yes, and in particular on the night of the storm. How was it you did not come?"

"Was there a storm?" she asked drowsily. "I must have slept, I did not hear it."

He now longed for her so intensely that he trembled with impatience. Her coolness inflamed his desperation.

"How can you be so cruel, Julia, and waste so much time?"

"I have never wasted a second's time," she said, entering the parlour, speaking over her shoulder. "I enjoy every moment of my existence. I told you before that you did not enter into it. Have you come begging and pleading for my favour?"

A last flare of pride made him deny this. He tried to go, but his feet were like lead and his spirit sank into a very woe of despondency at the thought of leaving her. There had been an ecstasy to wait for her when he was sure of her, but now that she so perpetually denied him, and he could see no good end to his delay, the thought of the loneliness of the Grange became insupportable.

He began to offer her high and reckless bribes.

"I will give you anything you ask for. You can have no idea, living as you do, what I am able to offer you."

"I only want one thing," said Miss Roseingrave, looking at him steadily, out of those black eyes whose glance he never could meet with complete composure, "and that, I think, you are in no mind to tender me."

"You do not know me," he protested. "I am never minded to cheapen a woman's favours."

"I perceive," she said, "that you misconceive me utterly. You will never get as much as a smile from me until I am your promised wife."

He was, at this, amazed to the swallowing up of all other possible emotions, and then he laughed, and opened his mouth as if to speak, then changed his mind. She stood very coolly waiting for his answer, but her glance was not indifferent.

"My wife. Now that's a strange request. Now that's a curious wish."

"It is my request and my wish. There are no other terms on which you get anything from me."

He was silent for a while and seemed to listen to the song of Phœbe coming from the upper room.

"I had not thought of it, but, as you will. My wife, then, and how soon?"

Julia Roseingrave strongly shuddered, as if his abrupt surrender brought more distress than delight.

"We will go away from here," she said. "I shall pay someone to look after my mother and Phœbe. We will go far away across the sea."

He shook his head.

"No, my dear, you belong here, to Holcot Grange. I should not care to see you transplanted. Dr. Rowland said you were like the foxgloves that died as soon as they were plucked or removed."

"Did you see Dr. Rowland, then?" she asked, very sharp,

"I rode over today and asked him if he knew of a spell to get you for me. But it seems that you are not so difficult. A mere wedding-ring—I might have thought of that myself."

"You'll take me away," she repeated. It was more like a command than an entreaty.

He shook his head again. For him she was one with Ballote Wood and the park and chestnut trees and the deserted Grange.

He would not dare to break the spell by taking her away. He, too, had his commands to give.

"You will marry me within a day or so and come and live with me at the Grange. You will do as I wish or I am like to prove an ill husband. And you must like me a little, too," he added, "for I will make no hollow bargain."

She answered, her voice was heavy with passion:

"Oh, William, I shall like you well enough."

He stepped towards her, but she raised her hand and such was the force of her gesture that she seemed to shut gates between them. "I am going upstairs to give my hour's reading to my mother. You can go to the church and have the banns called. Remember, when we are married I shall belong to you entirely, we can afford to wait."

Thus dismissed he left her, at once in an ecstasy and raging with deep pain.

XIII

Julia Roseingrave glided into the kitchen where Goody Cloke was making camomile tea.

"I have him, Mother Cloke, and without any of your spells," she whispered. "He has been here this afternoon and with very little ado promised to make me his wife. You see what I have gained by holding back. No town madam of great experience could have behaved with greater discretion."

"You are very clever, Miss Roseingrave," said Goody Cloke with admiration, "and I, poor old woman as I am, have helped a little."

"You shall be rewarded," said Miss Julia carelessly, "you shall be rewarded. I shall pay you good gold every week to stay here with my mother and sister while I go away."

"While you go away," echoed the old woman. "Do you think you are wise? You will give up such a deal when you leave Holcot Grange, will you not? All the places and the people, and the dreams."

"I shall see the world, Goody Cloke, for the first time. I shall ride in a carriage. I shall sleep in a gilt bed with vermilion curtains. I shall have diamonds to put round my throat and pearls to put in my ears, I shall have fine paints and unguents and powders to put upon my face and make myself a real beauty. I shall go where people admire me. I shall hear music and see dancing, I shall travel and behold many strange spectacles."

"Do you think you will be happy?" said the old woman, crushing the yellow flowers. "Do you really suppose that you will not find all those worldly pleasures brittle and hollow?"

"Sometimes I'm afraid so, sometimes I fear that I have lived here too long. I daresay I shall be homesick for the solitude. And there's the man himself, Mother Cloke, the man himself."

"Does he please you?" asked the old woman, pausing in her labour. The mangled daisies sent up an acrid perfume.

"Too well," said Miss Roseingrave, "too well."

XIV

It was their whim to be married in the little chapel of the Grange, which was to be cleaned and furnished for the occasion. Mrs. Barlow and the maids worked diligently to scour and polish.

The gardens were searched for trophies of the late summer to deck the altar. There was not much to be found, only late marigolds, St. Michael's daisies, and a few spears of tawny lilies.

"Not like bridal flowers," grumbled Mrs. Barlow, who disliked the marriage and the bride, and had nothing but fear for the bridegroom. It was all ill-omened, she said, and seemed more like the fulfilling of the curse on the Grange than anything else, and unnatural that Sir William should be married in this hole-and-corner fashion so far from his friends and his usual company.

And as for Julia Roseingrave, no one had ever imagined that she would marry at all. A sly, ambitious hussy she must have been, Mrs. Barlow thought, who had waited patiently with her air of decorum and virtue for so long, ready to pounce on the first likely man who came her way. And lucky she had been to have found such a chance as that of a marriage with Sir William Notley!

Miss Roseingrave had few preparations to make for her marriage. As soon as she was Sir William's wife she intended to leave Holcot Grange and all the surrounding country, and leave it for ever. But at the present moment, a certain sloth and languor enveloped her, and she could not endure to make the long journey necessary to procure herself a fine wedding gown.

She therefore turned over the ancient garments belonging to her mother that she had stored in a press in her bedchamber. These were tarnished, and some even rent. She discovered one of rich white silk which greatly took her fancy, but it fell to pieces in her hand. So she resolved to be married in the gown of cowslip-coloured silk embroidered with the purple black violets.

What did it matter?—the few who would be present at her wedding knew her so well that she could not hope to impress them. And her bridegroom would care little what her garments were.

Three days before her wedding day she sat at the window sewing ruffles, which Mother Cloke had washed, mended and ironed, on to the wrists and bosom of this gown. Her mother lay on a couch in this same chamber and regarded her daughter secretly from under the shade of her frilled cambric cap.

Miss Roseingrave believed that her mother understood very well all about her marriage. She had told her in clear, deliberate tones and a slight convulsion had passed over the paralysed face of the dumb woman, as if she understood that she was to be left to the care of the herb woman while her daughter went far away out into the varying world that she herself had left so long ago.

Phœbe certainly had understood, for her mind had been quite clear of late, as it often was for months together, and when she heard that her sister was going away she had danced and clapped her hands above her head, upon which Miss Roseingrave had smiled at Mother Cloke, who had said: "Ungrateful, and after all your kindness."

"Those poor, simple creatures read the heart," replied Miss Julia calmly, "and I have never felt any kindness to her nor to my mother. Indeed, I often wonder what induced me to spend such long years with these two poor wretches."

Looking up now from her fine sewing Miss Julia smiled and nodded across the green shade of the room. The chamber had a look as if it were under water by reason of the shadows of the trees without.

"Are you glad, Mother, that I am making this splendid and marvellous match and going far away? Perhaps you, like Phœbe, would clap your hands if you had the use of them, to be rid of me. It will make little difference to you, I think, whether or no I am gone, for the herb woman will look after you quite well."

But though the words in themselves were gentle and even affectionate, Miss Julia's looks at the afflicted woman were keen and even mocking and Mrs. Roseingrave dropped her eyelids and again that convulsion passed over her distorted face, as if she felt, like a stab in the heart, the harsh unkindness of her daughter.

There was a knock at the door, and Miss Julia's smooth, triumphant face clouded.

"That is Sir William, and I told him not to come. I shall be staled in his regard before we are married," she added vexedly, and put down her sewing and descended the small stairs.

It was not her lover who stood under the ripening berries of the woodbine, but a stranger and a woman.

"Are you Miss Roseingrave?"

The accents were timid and accompanied by a gesture of clasped hands, almost like a supplication.

"I am she, madam."

"Then perhaps you will let me come into your house. This is the Dower House of Holcot Grange, is it not?"

"It is so, madam."

"Let me come into your house," pursued the stranger with an increasing difficulty, as if she were faint and exhausted, "to speak to you a little while. Perhaps, too, you will give me shelter for the night, for I have nowhere else to go."

"Madam, there is an inn in the village," said Miss Roseingrave, courteously, but not moving from the open door, "and it is not so many miles, and an easy walk through the shadows of the woods."

"I do not wish to go there," said the stranger, in a low and humble voice; "I want a woman's support and succour. I have travelled a long way today and I am very fatigued. I pray you, of your charity, allow me a little repose in your parlour."

At that, Miss Roseingrave stood aside, and the other woman passed her with a deep sigh. She was young and very fair. There was dust on her shoes and bonnet. She walked heavily and Julia Roseingrave felt a ready contempt for her as she motioned her into the parlour where a large jar of tall foxgloves with spotted throats wide open and half-bursting seed pods hanging from the lower portion of the stems, stood in the centre of the table.

Miss Roseingrave offered the exhausted stranger a seat, and at the same time told her briefly that she was burdened with the care of an invalid mother and an imbecile sister, and was herself occupied with preparations for sudden departure, therefore she feared, whatever the lady's circumstances, she could be of little help.

"Yes, I know about your mother and sister, Miss Roseingrave," said the stranger meekly. "I was told about them at a cottage where

I inquired, and that is really why I came to you. I thought that you must be a very good and gentle woman, living here so long with such a task. 'Surely,' I said to myself, 'this lady will help me.' But I shall not long trespass on your time or your good humour. Holcot Grange is my destination, and I should not in any case have delayed here long."

"Holcot Grange," repeated Miss Roseingrave, peering at the other behind the topmost spikes of the foxgloves.

"Yes, the truth is, Miss Roseingrave, that I have come to speak to my husband."

"Madam, you will not find him at the Grange. This is a very solitary place."

"Oh," exclaimed the lady, in a tone of deep disappointment, and rising in her agitation, "did not Sir William Notley come here a few weeks ago?"

"Yes, madam, Sir William Notley, but you said your husband?"

"Sir William is my husband," said the lady.

Miss Roseingrave remained rigid, peering through the topmost branch of the foxgloves.

A sudden panic of unnameable terror set the other woman crying out. It was like the impotent buzzing of a fly who realises that he is caught in the web.

"Oh, I will go, I beg you not to concern yourself! Indeed, I was distracted, or I should not have disturbed you! I will go at once to the Grange."

She tried to escape from the room, but Miss Roseingrave moved swiftly before the door.

"It were better for all of us, madam, if you were to tell me your story first. Perhaps, indeed, I can help you."

"I would rather be gone," protested the other, but Miss Roseingrave dominated her without much trouble, and motioned her back to the chintz seat in the window-place, and bade her tell her tale.

"I have been married five years, Miss Roseingrave, and we have two little children. He certainly has neglected me very much of late, and been wild and getting into bad company and I have been unhappy. But he is my husband always, and the man whom I love, and when he fled from town some weeks ago I could not endure it but must make enquiries as to his whereabouts. There was a friend of his who was in his confidence, and who would solace me, and told me where he was, but said I had best leave him alone, so I wrote several times and had no answer. Then I thought how strange and dreadful it was that he should be so far away and I know nothing of what was happening to him. So I decided to come to Holcot Grange and find him for myself."

"Perhaps he is repentant," said Miss Roseingrave.

"Ah, I should not use that word, it is cruel. And, after all, he did little harm on the night of the masquerade. It was another who struck the fatal blow."

"Does anyone know that you have come here, Lady Notley?" asked Miss Roseingrave.

"Indeed no, madam, I dared tell none, for I knew that all would endeavour to prevent me, so I came secretly and travelled without incident. I have plenty of money. I left the coach three hours ago, and have been walking ever since. I had only to enquire my way once."

"Why did you not, madam, go directly to the Grange?"

"I do not know. My courage failed me, I suppose. He can be very violent and dreadful. And I believe," the tears lay in her gentle eyes, "that he has long since ceased to care much for me, Miss Roseingrave. Perhaps he will resent that I have followed him, and so I asked if there was any about here with whom I could stay a little first to repose myself, and you were named."

"You have done well, Lady Notley," said Miss Roseingrave. "It is true that Sir William is at the Grange, and has lived there very quietly, and seen no one but Mr. Morley of Griffinshaws, the steward. I know nothing at all of his history, and indeed have seen him but seldom, and I shall be very pleased if you will come up to my room and rest. I will make you a dish of tea and you may bathe your hands and face and raise your spirits before you visit your husband."

Lady Notley thanked Miss Roseingrave warmly and went upstairs eagerly enough, for indeed she was much fatigued, both by hard and unusual travelling and by the alternate elation and depression of her spirits. With a sigh of relief she stretched herself on Miss Roseingrave's narrow bed with the dimity coverlet, and, expressing her deep thankfulness for so much kindness, was soon asleep.

Miss Roseingrave looked at her keenly. She was a very fair woman, and if she were happy, might indeed be most beautiful.

Miss Roseingrave opened the bag that the strange lady had brought with her and found within it a miniature of Sir William Notley, a little packet of love letters, several rings, plenty of money, and two little drawings of young children in a book made of white satin.

Miss Roseingrave put all these objects carefully back in their place and went downstairs to the kitchen, where Mother Cloke was crimping and goffering a white dress for Phœbe to wear on the wedding-day.

"Mother Cloke," said Miss Roseingrave, carefully closing the kitchen door, "his wife has come searching for him. She is upstairs asleep now. They have two children."

"His wife?" said Mother Cloke, in a whistling whisper. "Why, it is some impostor, surely."

"She is too much a baby fool to be an impostor," said Miss Julia. "I am a fool, too. I should have known from the readiness with which he agreed to our marriage that I was being deceived."

Mother Cloke was frightened by her calmness.

"He is indeed a wicked man, Miss Roseingrave. You have been sorely deceived. What are you going to do?"

"She is wholly in my power," said Miss Julia calmly. "Though you could not help me to a love potion, Goody Cloke, I suppose there is another matter in which you could assist very well."

The glances of the two women met, then Mother Cloke said, fearfully:

"Hush, Miss Phœbe is in the closet, eating cherry preserve, which I have given her to keep her quiet. She will have overheard every word of what we have said."

"What does that matter, Goody Cloke? She understands nothing."

But the herb woman was frightened, for she knew that the idiot girl did very often understand quite well what was said. In the rest of her conversation with Miss Roseingrave she lowered her voice, the two of them bending close together over the table, where lay the dainty piles of clear starched and goffered frocks and aprons and caps.

XV

Phœbe Roseingrave was unnaturally swift and tireless. She could run, the villagers said, as fast as a hare, and they were often frightened to see how quickly she sped across the meadows and the marsh.

This afternoon, with smears of cherry preserve still on her lips and fingers she fled through the sunlight to the oasthouse where Dr. Rowland lived. Once or twice she paused, completely forgetting her errand, and was distracted by the chasing of a mouse through the dry grasses or the sound of a skylark singing high above her head. But always there came back into her mind what she had to do, and when she arrived at the oasthouse, she was quite clear about her message.

"Why, poor Phœbe," said Dr. Rowland as he admitted her. "It is a long time since I have seen you. Now, what brought you here all through the heat?"

And then she again forgot what she had to say and began to gibber and grimace, so he thought that this uncommon visit was but a whim of her imbecility and gave her a pack of cards to play with and went upstairs to his laboratory.

Phœbe lay on the floor in the square patch of sunlight that fell through the high windows and played with the cards which were covered with strange devices, in red, green and yellow. She looked like Miss Julia Roseingrave when she lay there, long, slim, and graceful, with a swathe of black hair falling over her shoulders and her straight featured, pale face.

Then she remembered why she had run away into the empty afternoon. She sprang up and called up the ladder staircase: "Dr. Rowland! Dr. Rowland!" So that he opened the top door and looked down, wiping his fingers on the leathern apron that he used when he was making his experiments.

"Oh, Dr. Rowland," said Miss Phœbe, slyly, "Julia and Mother Cloke are making the foxglove tea for the strange lady who came this afternoon."

"And who is the strange lady, my poor child?"

Phœbe grinned, showing her pale gums and long teeth.

"She is Sir William Notley's wife, and Julia was going to marry him."

"Ah, yes, Julia is going to be married in two days' time," frowned Dr. Rowland. "It had gone out of my head, it does not matter very much. I suppose it means she will go away, I shall certainly miss her."

"But the wife has come, the wife has come!" said Phœbe, dancing round in the patch of sunlight on the bright faces of the fallen cards.

"You wild, mad thing," said Dr. Rowland, "you are not telling the truth."

"The truth, the truth!" shrieked Phœbe, leaping like poor Wat in the moonlight, and she opened the door and tore away across the sunny silence.

Dr. Rowland stood thoughtfully at the top of the ladder stairway.

"If such a thing should be true, would Julia act like that? And if she intended to act like that, should I wish to prevent it? What will it matter one way or another? We shall all be dust ere the least of the stars have twinkled twice," and he closed the door and went back to his experiments.

XVI

Miss Roseingrave and Mother Cloke were so occupied that afternoon that they did not notice the absence of Phœbe nor how, when she came home, she crept upstairs to her sister's bedroom and gaped long and curiously at the stranger, heavily asleep on the dimity-covered bed, and after that went to where her mother lay and whispered to her long and eagerly.

Although Miss Julia was not aware of the fact, these two understood each other perfectly. Mrs. Roseingrave could use her left hand a little and shape a few characters on paper, though with difficulty. A pencil usually lay within her reach and she contrived to get hold of this, when Phœbe had finished her chatter, and to write with painful effort a few words on a fly-leaf she tore out of the Bible. It took her some time to accomplish this task, and Phœbe gaped at her the while without offering to help.

What Mrs. Roseingrave had written was: "Your wife is here," and the name of Sir William Notley.

She pushed this paper into Phœbe's hands and tried to convey to her that she was to deliver it to the Baronet. Phœbe ran out of the room as if she had understood, but no sooner had she left her mother's presence than she forgot all about the paper and went out into the park, chasing the blue butterflies she saw flying under the chestnut trees, and in this frantic pursuit the paper fell out of her bosom, where she had tucked it, on to the path which led to Holcot Grange.

So that Sir William, coming towards the Dower House at the hour of sunset saw the paper, picked it up, and read the message.

XVII

Sir William went on steadily towards the Dower House. His startled thoughts had at first leapt in amaze, but afterwards it seemed to him that if his wife had followed him it were but a reasonable thing and what he should have expected. He ought to have known the lengths to which her fidelity, devotion, and innocent affection would drive her. When he had burnt her letters, one after another, holding them in a candle, and watching with delight the thin paper curl, he ought to have realised he would not be rid of her so easily.

And now she was at the Dower House and in the power of Julia Roseingrave. Julia must know by now his deception. Had she herself written the message in the uncouth characters and thrown it where he was sure to meet it on his path? How would she take this strange turn, but two days off her wedding? His mood became dark, sullen, and dangerous. He had planned it all so neatly, and all had gone so smoothly. Why should he have supposed that in this remote place any evil chance would find him out? But he knew only too well that there was no hiding from destiny.

When he came in sight of the brick façade of the house with the ripening woodbine over the door and the last carnations blowing sweetly in the neat garden, he vowed in his soul that come what may he would not lose Julia Roseingrave and he felt a deep anger against his innocent wife, who, in a folly of love, had thus thwarted his designs.

Miss Julia did not come at once when he knocked, but when she did open the door to him her face was stormy and her greeting cold.

"I told you to stay away from me till our wedding-day," she said.

"I could not, Julia, I love you too much. You are in my thoughts day and night. You come between me and sleep."

She allowed him to enter the parlour. The foxgloves were gone from the table. As she seated herself in a haughty and displeased acquiescence in his presence, he saw at once that she was not going to tell him of her visitor. She, then, had not written the paper, and he wondered what he should do. His mood became, like hers, exasperated and dangerous.

She fenced with him for a little while, talking of indifferent matters and basing her coldness and her displeasure on his breaking of the rule she had laid down that he was not to try to see her till their wedding morning. But her arts were of little avail with him. All the course of his licentious and lawless life he had not been used to intrigue or to subtle meanings, so he broke bluntly and impatiently through her fine and delicate sentences.

"I found this on my path just now, Julia, as I came through the chestnut trees. Is it a trick or a jest?" and he held out to her the fly-leaf of the Bible on which was painfully traced the message from the paralytic woman.

Miss Julia Roseingrave betrayed herself by a hot flush of anger, and a quiver in her voice in which she said:

"Who dared write that? Did Phœbe, after all, understand?"

"My wife is here, then," said Sir William Notley, coldly, returning the paper to his breast pocket, "now, why did you conceal that from me, Julia?"

"Why did you conceal from me that you had a wife at all?" she demanded passionately. Then, staying his reply, with a contemptuous gesture she answered herself:

"But I should know you thought I was a rustic fool, to be easily caught and so I was such a fool and so caught."

"Why should you think," he demanded scornfully, "that I was not married? Did you think at my age with my rank that I should be still free? And if I had been, do you suppose that I should have married you?"

"I had very little experience," said Miss Roseingrave, "and I was deceived."

"I do not believe you," he said. "It suited you to pretend to be deceived."

"Leave it like that, then, Sir William, it matters very little now. I have been saved in time."

"Saved from me, do you mean? Indeed, Julia, you do not know what you are talking about. The fact that this poor foolish woman has come here will make no difference, none at all. I must and will have you."

She smiled without answering, and maddened by her coldness, he added:

"If you wish for the wedding to deceive those about here, let us have it, and on some excuse I will send this poor fool back to the city."

"She will not go," said Miss Roseingrave. "She loves you. I wonder why? You are a worthless man."

"Do not you love me, Julia?"

"I intend to marry you," she replied, and he was angered that she should be such a powerful magnet of attraction to him, when he could get no confession of passion from her cool lips.

This sudden and unexpected obstacle caused by the arrival of his wife further inflamed his wild illicit desire for Julia Roseingrave, a desire that seemed to him like a fever, something not quite normal nor quite sane, so that sometimes it seemed to him that she had indeed bewitched him or cast some spell upon his senses.

It was not love, this passion, and sometimes it was near to hate. Now, as he sat quite close to her in the neat, overcrowded parlour he felt a sensation of repulsion—a desire to escape from the room, the house, the company of the woman; he felt that beneath all this parade of decorum and prudery there lay some trap, and again he seemed to hear that high, thin voice calling a warning.

His sight seemed affected and he struggled against the hallucination that the room was full of phantoms, moving, tall grey figures who came and went, and circled round and about the erect lovely shape, and cold smooth face of Miss Julia Roseingrave.

"The strain is intolerable," he muttered, "and I detest this place. We must get away. What does it matter about my wife? She can return as she came."

"Have you no care at all, then, for her safety? Is not her dignity and honour something involved in yours?"

"I cannot think about that now. She has her own relatives. She is a woman who will take care of herself, she is very nice and fastidious."

He scarcely knew what he said.

"She is sleeping upstairs," said Miss Roseingrave, "would you like to go and see her?"

"No, no," he said violently.

"She has brought with her your portrait, and that of your children. She seems a good, sweet, gentle fool."

"I never wish to see her again. She must not come between you and me, Julia."

"She has come. She is your wife, and I, as I told you before, will not belong to you on any other terms than that of marriage."

He felt impotent before her, corrupt and debased even from his own low standard. He had already understood her meaning and cried out in rage, because the solution that she now offered to him was unescapable and inevitable, was one that had come to him when he picked up the letter on the path under the chestnut trees, and one, too, that he had rejected with instantaneous horror, and now, in a sudden flash of terror, he saw that what Miss Julia Roseingrave proposed was not by any means to be rejected or slighted. He was in her snare, he could not lose her nor slight her...

"No one knows she is here," said Miss Julia Roseingrave, speaking quietly, with her hands folded in her lap. And she related to his sullen silence the tale that Lady Notley had related.

"I should have expected it. I daresay her letters that I destroyed gave me some warning of it," he said, with dull fury. "But I did not wish to break the enchantment. Yes, it is as if I had been under an enchantment here. I want to forget her and all the old life."

And then, undisciplined and fickle, violent and sudden as he was, he began to struggle against his destiny, which he read clearly enough in the lustrous dark eyes of Julia Roseingrave.

"Cannot we go away together, you and I, and leave the poor fool alone? I shall never look at her again if you are jealous of her."

"Jealous," interrupted Julia, "not I!"

"Will nothing please you," he pleaded, "but to be my wife? I must have you and that you know. But here is a price I would never pay. Had this fond wretch never come to interrupt us I would have married you and you would have been my wife for all you had known. We would have gone abroad together."

"You babble nonsense," she interrupted. "I should have found out and quite soon. As soon as I had left these solitudes and gone into the world the truth would have been manifest and then I should have hated you, and perhaps I should have—"

She paused, but he understood what she would have said.

"I daresay you know a few dangerous secrets," he muttered. "You mean that you would have revenged yourself on me."

"I want," she said, "some of the prizes and honours of the world or nothing. I have been content in this desolation, for I have had sharp and sweet dreams, and if you take those from me you must give me something else. I shall be your wife and mistress of all you own, or I shall remain here, forgetting you quite easily and live as I lived before, on phantoms."

"You talk and talk but to torment me, for you know that I cannot forgo you. I believe that you have given me some potion to drink." Then he broke off and asked distractedly: "What do you intend to do? We are in a far corner of the world here, but, remember, we are still in it. Do nothing that will put you in peril."

"I shall do nothing at all," she said; "it was all in my hands and I intended to settle it by myself. I and Goody Cloke. Now you have interfered you may take it on to yourself."

"I?" he asked, and terror flashed in his eyes. "You want me to do it?"

"Why, certainly. If you want me it should not be so much to you to destroy what comes between us."

"To destroy!" he echoed.

"Well, perhaps you are sorry for her!" mocked Miss Roseingrave. "Perhaps you think of your two young children and all she had endured for your sake, the tender, innocent love she still bears for you. Well, if these things influence you, you may go upstairs and take her by the hand and go on your knees and beg her to forgive you, and go away with her and leave me here alone."

"You know," he muttered in agony, "that I cannot do this. You and I are bound together, by some horrid mischance, perhaps, Julia, but bound together none the less. And if marriage is the only way—"

"Nothing else concerns me," she said. "I wish to be Lady Notley."

And he laughed because her intention and her words sat grotesquely together. And behind his own voice he heard again and very faintly, the shrill warning echo.

"She need not suffer," he said sullenly.

"Why, no, Mother Cloke is very skilful. She will make a cordial that you shall give her and that will set her at rest for ever."

"I cannot do it, Julia. I cannot see her, and do this."

"You must. I desire you to do it. There is no escape. It must be quickly before anyone knows that she is here."

Miss Roseingrave rose and approached him, speaking in a low, rapid whisper, that he listened to, fascinated as if indeed this were an incantation that she wove about his excited and bewildered senses.

He had an even deeper impression than before, that mysterious figures wove a mystic dance round about her and that the small, neat parlour was crowded with menacing phantoms.

"She will wake presently and I shall go up to her, and say that I have sent a message to the Grange, telling you of her arrival here and bidding you come. And then she will be soothed and calmed and I shall help her to make herself neat. She will come down and receive you here, and I shall come in as the pleasant, agreeable hostess and hand you a drink that you must not touch yourself but give to her. Then all will be over quite suddenly."

"Why should you put this on to me? Why should you not take this terrible sin on your own head and hands? You gain the prize."

He spoke thickly, from a wilderness of dreams, pressed on him very closely.

"Prize!" she cried. "Am I no prize?"

And overpowered by the force of her and the strong truth of what she said, he went down on his knees and buried his face in the thin silk cushion, stuffed with hops for drowsiness, that lay on the little sofa.

"Never mind for what comes after," she said, standing erect over him. "What troubled sleep or restless dreams or flat disappointment. We have made our bargain and resolved to put it through. And shall this poor, slight thing come between us? And it can be done so easily."

He looked up at her, his face haggard between the fallen dark locks.

"And afterwards?"

"Afterwards it will be so easy," said she, swiftly understanding him. "You and I and Mother Cloke will take her out after it is dark and down to Ballote Wood. There has been a long drought, but the rain will come soon. Mother Cloke says so and she is always right—the pond, where you saw me bathing—"

"It was you, then?" he asked dully.

"Who should it be but I? That pond is nearly dry now, the lily roots are all exposed to the sun and rotting. There we may easily dig—the ground is soft, and anything placed there would sink immediately. And afterwards, when the rain comes, all will be hidden, and the lilies will grow again and no one will ever go searching near there for the place is supposed to be haunted."

Miss Roseingrave lifted her lip at his silence.

"Could she have a better end? It is pleasanter for her this way than to live married to you."

Then, as he did not move, she added:

"You are very faint-hearted. Is this worse than other things that you have done?"

He rose to his feet and tried to menace her.

"Why should I not have my own way? Why should you plan this for me? You are fixing a dark stain on my soul that I shall never efface. This place is indeed cursed and haunted."

He began to rave and to lament. She placed a cool, long hand on his arm, and bade him be silent, and then he shuddered with a baser fear.

"Have we been overheard? You trust Mother Cloke, you say? Why should we? Is it safe?"

"I will answer for her," said Miss Roseingrave.

But his mean terror was not to be assuaged so easily. "And the letter? Who dropped the letter in my path?"

"That must be some trick on the part of Phœbe," she frowned. "The girl is an idiot, and even if she should speak she will not be listened to."

Sir William said: "I never thought to be so under anyone's domination as I am under yours. The time will come when your spell will break and I shall loathe you."

He would have said more and fallen to raging again, but she stemmed the torrent of his words by saying coldly:

"Begone, and come again about nine o'clock when it is quite dark."

And he left her and returned to Holcot Grange.

XVIII

The young man, alone in the empty house, brooded over what he was about to do. An extraordinary change had fallen over the empty apartments, the garden, and the landscape. He could not blame himself for his wickedness, for he was involved in a *miasma* of evil which penetrated into his veins with every breath he drew.

All fresh fragrance had gone from the trees, and all perfumed beauty from the flowers. Everything was of a rancid yellow or a withered brown—rotting, corrupting, and rank.

As he had wandered by the *quidnunc* he had found a dead dove in his path and swarms of poisonous flies glimmered round the unwholesome seeds of exotic plants. The sky was a dull, sulphurous colour and there was not the slightest stir of wind.

The phantoms that he had noticed with such terror in the Dower House accompanied him to the Grange. They all, he thought, seemed aware of his diabolic purpose; he half believed them to be but the projections of his own delirium, and half feared they were the attendants of Julia Roseingrave sent to encompass him with demoniacal promptings until he had done her bidding.

He felt utterly exhausted and the exasperation of his disappointed desire put him out of harmony with everything, as suddenly as, a short while before, he had felt at one with the universe. Then, all had been smooth, now all was ajar. His misery was acute.

He wandered away to gaze in the chapel, where all was now complete for his accursed marriage. He realised that she would be his wife in very truth, not that mock bride that he had desired her to be. He could not peer into the future at all nor speculate on how long they would stay together, nor what their joint actions would be nor where they would go.

He shuddered at the thought of what she had bid him do, and, on the verge of delirium as he was, he saw his wife's eyes looking at him meekly, with an inexpressible tenderness and lustrous with tears.

Yet he knew that he could neither disobey nor forgo Julia Roseingrave.

The future was to him so dark and full of menace, yet it was shot with a hope of a dreadful joy. Surely, in the possession of that woman he would know some such ecstasy as he had hitherto only touched in the phantasmagoria of dreams.

Yet as he waited under this strain and terror for the dark to fall, which would be the signal for him to go again to the Dower House, he thought of Miss Roseingrave almost with repugnance, and his mind, on the verge of complete overthrow, began to dwell on the question as to how long he should support her company.

She had largely won him by withholding herself so completely. Once she was completely his he might quickly tire, and he resolved with half-insane cunning that he would obtain from her the secret of Mother Cloke's potion, and take one with him on his wedding journey, and as soon as he had tired of her perverse and poisonous beauty, administer to her the same quietus for life's fever that she proposed to give his wife.

His wife!

His broken and distracted thoughts hung about that word, and he thought of Blanche as she had been when he had first married her five years ago. So gay and charming and unsuspecting of evil, so fond and gracious! How soon he had tired of her tender affections, of her insipid talk, and shallow mind!

He began to consider the lily pond where he had first seen Julia Roseingrave bathing. Now, another tress of hair, this time pale, would float upon what was left of the stagnant water, and another face more deadly white even than that of Miss Roseingrave would show for a while between the lily roots.

It was all very cleverly contrived; never would he be suspected. Those who had missed his wife from the city might think a thousand times before they would fall upon the truth. Probably they would consider that the fond wretch must have drowned herself because she had loved and been forsaken.

Dimly there came to him the thought of his two little children, but this moved him not at all.

At sunset the spell on him deepened, and when Mrs. Barlow came to set his last meal before him, she was frightened at his face, so scowling was he with his head thrust forward from his hunched-up shoulders.

How changed, she thought, from the man she had seen unmasked for the first time when she had brought Mr. Morley of Griffinshaws into his presence some weeks ago! Yet even then she had thought his aspect dreadful.

In silence she laid out his food and wine. She was rather glad that he did not speak to her, yet his dumbness frightened her, too. And she wished that the Vicar lived nearer, that she might send one of the servant girls for him and bid him come over and keep her master company that night.

She thought to herself as she hurried from the Grange to the servants' quarters:

"This is an accursed marriage. Surely it is bringing a disaster with it."

Sir William could not touch any of his food. Indeed, he scarcely saw it was there, but he rose up from the undisturbed table and went into the little parlour where he had first seen Mother Cloke with her basket of herbs and tried to play on the various instruments. But he found those that were stringed had all the cords snapped and those that were keyed were out of tune and jarred horribly when he touched them. And as he stood among all this ruined music, he realised that the day was darkening down and that soon it would be time for him to go to the Dower House. And all the phantoms seemed to crowd up close about him, pressing on his lips and bosom until he could scarcely breathe.

And he thought: "This is the doom of all my evil life. It is now useless to think of escape."

XIX

Dr. Rowland's experiment had failed. There was nothing in the bottom of the crucible, that should have held flakes of pure gold, but a little evil-smelling deposit.

He laughed at himself, then damped his furnaces, locked the door of his laboratory and went out into the evening air.

A melancholy light was diffused over the far horizon. The delicate glow of evening diffused the dry September landscape into a semblance of beauty.

It was a long time since Doctor Rowland had left his laboratory or given much thought to anything besides his experiments. Now that the last of these had failed, his interest in worldly affairs revived, and he thought with delight of Julia Roseingrave, and of the long hours which he would, for a space, spend in her company. And how she would comfort him in his disappointment, and how he would discuss with her fresh efforts to be made in the future.

And then he recalled, as idly he watched some thistledown seeds blow across his path, that Julia Roseingrave was to be married and would go away, leaving him quite desolate.

"Why that," he said, half aloud, "would overthrow me quite."

And he wondered at what manner of trance he had been in, so to overlook this great misfortune, and he recalled the coming of Phœbe.

Had it been today, or yesterday, or the day before? What had she said? "Sir William's wife has come back and Julia and Mother

Cloke are going to give her the foxglove tea." There was no trust to be put in anything that the idiot might say. But that did not concern him. He must keep Julia for himself.

He returned to his stable and saddled his willing horse, which yearned for the road after too long a stabling, and rode briskly to Holcot Grange.

He arrived there when the dusk had settled into complete dark. He had never been to the deserted Grange before, and he never thought of using the large front gates, but went instead to the servants' entrance and left his horse there, and Mrs. Barlow brought him into the Grange by the side door, which she used herself, and so into the presence of Sir William as he was leaving the music-room, with an intent look as one drawn by a lodestone against his will, to go through the park and under the chestnut trees to the Dower House where both his wife and Julia Roseingrave waited for him. The young man did not recognise his visitor and made a movement to pass him, as if, indeed, he were not there. But Dr. Rowland detained him by taking him strongly by the wrist, drawing him into the room where all the broken musical instruments stood, and one lamp burnt in the window-place.

"Where are you going, Sir William Notley? To visit Miss Roseingrave?"

"That is my destination," replied the other in a muffled voice. "And who are you, for indeed I cannot recall your features? But whoever you are," he added, with impatience, "you must not interrupt nor impede me now, I have serious business to do."

"You look disordered," said Dr. Rowland, spying at him deeply from behind his silver-rimmed spectacles, "and as if you were weighed down by dead sins and a debauched mind. Your pulse beats too fast and I think you are fevered. It were better for you to leave Julia Roseingrave alone."

"I am to marry her, in two days' time," and like one who has conned a lesson, the young man repeated, "two days' time, in two days' time I am to be married to Julia Roseingrave."

"No," said Dr. Rowland, flinging away from him with a movement of contempt the young man's hot hand, which until now he had held in his own, "you're going to do nothing of the kind. I should have stopped this before. But I have been busy with an experiment which has, alas, come to nothing."

"You will stop my marriage?"

"Miss Roseingrave is mine," said Dr. Rowland. "How do you think that we have, either of us, endured this solitude, if we did not belong one to another? Whatever feeling you may have for her, or she for you, it is but visionary and transitory, she and I are together in this landscape, in this place, and always will be. You cannot remove her."

"You are some demon or devil in disguise, seeking to thwart me!"

"Say, perhaps, rather your good angel," smiled Dr. Rowland. "Do you think that you would taste any joys at all with a woman like Miss Roseingrave? Fie, for shame, what nonsensical notion have you allowed to get the possession of you? Has she put a spell on you?" he added, with a peering look. "I did not think that she was clever enough for that."

"A spell, a spell," repeated the young man dully. He sat down by one of the viols with the snapped strings and took his face in his hands.

"Don't you understand," said Dr. Rowland, in a fashion not unkindly. "She belongs to me and has done so ever since she was a young girl."

"Are you married to her?" asked Sir William.

"If you like to believe it! There was a ceremony with a hedge priest down in the marsh and the guests were a motley and a curious crowd. We have never avowed a union."

"You lie," said Sir William, heavily struggling to his feet, "I must go to her. She has commanded me. She has appointed something for me to do."

Dr. Rowland's manner was now cold and ferocious.

"Have you become lunatic with fond and idle imaginings and unrestrained fancies? Do you not see that the net of the devil is about you? Even if you be something of a fiend yourself, a larger demon has you in his power. What, do you want to act like an idiot or a child? Be precise, tell me what has happened. Maybe I can save you. Knowing her I should have foreseen this peril," he added in a more gentle tone.

"But as I say, I have been absorbed."

Sir William laid his hands on Dr. Rowland's shoulders, and said in the voice of a child confessing a small fault:

"She has my wife there—my true wife, and she has commanded me to destroy her tonight. Which can very easily be done, and I am not afraid of telling you, for no one would believe your word against mine."

Dr. Rowland took off his spectacles and out of his tired, bloodshot eyes stared at the young man with a great compassion. Sir William melted before this look and sighed:

"Save me, if you can, from what I am about to do, for I cannot save myself. A while ago I was without hope, but now I am dimly conscious that there is help coming."

Dr. Rowland put his hand into the bosom of his old-fashioned habit and drew out a crucifix.

"This is no use to me, but may be to you," he said. "Hold it tightly in your hand, and do not stir from this room until I return."

As Sir William, clasping the sacred symbol, sank in the window-place beside the solitary lamp, Dr. Rowland turned through the sultry night under the yellow chestnut trees towards the Dower House.

He found Julia Roseingrave sewing the ruffles to the dress that was the colour of cowslips, embroidered with blue-black violets.

She scowled when she saw that it was Dr. Rowland, and not Sir William Notley, who brusquely entered the parlour.

"How is it I did not know you before, you wicked, foolish woman?" he pondered quietly.

She shrank away from him and her sewing dropped from her fingers.

"Have you been trying spells and charms, incantations and witcheries?" he demanded, harshly, approaching her.

"No, master, no!" She shook her head. "I wanted to get away, that was only natural, was it not?"

"You know that you'll never get away. You are here for ever. And now I shall leave you."

She began to whimper.

"Oh, not that! Not that! I did not really mean to be unfaithful. I should soon have left him. It was only that I wanted a chance of seeing the great varied world. I meant to be rid of him."

"With your foxglove potion, I suppose," he interrupted; with a quick movement of his strong hands he knocked over a white glass of cordial that stood on a tray on the table in the spot where the foxgloves had been. "You and your stupid womanish tricks! All of them learnt from me and misunderstood in the learning. I thought just now," he said, with some sorrow, "that I could not endure to lose you. My experiments failed and I thought of you when my mind was empty, and I went up to Holcot Grange, to tell the young man that you were mine—that you *were* mine—I have no part in you now. Then I found what you had done to him."

"It is nothing, master! It is nothing!" she sighed. "Whatever he said to you was a lie—a lie!"

"Oh, no, he was already an outcast from Heaven, but you, gorgeously tricked out with all the delights of the senses, were going to make him an inhabitant of Hell."

Julia Roseingrave began to weep. Dr. Rowland took his spectacles from his pocket, wiped them, and placed them on the bridge of his high nose.

"Where is this woman, his lady wife?" he asked.

And Miss Roseingrave said: "Upstairs. But he will never take her back. He belongs to me, I tell you."

Dr. Rowland made no answer to this, but went up the narrow stairway. The door of Mrs. Roseingrave's room stood open.

She lay there, no more rigid than usual, and not much paler than usual, but Dr. Rowland's one glance told him that the woman was dead. He was glad of this, but he said nothing to Phœbe, who lay stretched on the ground beside the corpse, playing, by the light of the candle, with a large wooden doll.

At the door of Julia's bedroom he knocked respectfully. It was almost instantly opened, and Lady Notley stood within, her face newly bathed, her hair newly combed, all radiant and expectant.

"Your husband cannot come to you tonight," he said, "but I have come to fetch you to him."

"He is not angry?" whispered the lady fearfully.

"No, he is not angry with anyone save himself."

She trusted this strange-looking man and turned back in the room to fetch her small bag, in which lay her few treasures, and followed him down the stairs and out through the door under the ripening woodbine.

As they left the house a long wail of despair smote their ears. Lady Notley shuddered.

"It is that poor idiot," she breathed fearfully. But Dr. Rowland knew that it was not Phœbe but Julia who had wailed.

XX

The moon rose when Dr. Rowland brought Lady Notley across the park to Holcot Grange, the sultry mists dispersed. The lady trembled greatly as she came nearer and nearer to her husband's presence and began to lament her daring in undertaking this journey which she was sure was against his wish and in a manner forcing herself into the presence of one whom she dared swear had forgotten her.

"But I do it for my children's sake," she said, "and a little, too, for his own, for there is none other save myself who really cares to save him."

"To save him from what, Lady Notley?" asked Dr. Rowland kindly.

"To save him from all those evils that crowd about him."

"Sincere love can do much," said Dr. Rowland. "We so few of us have the strength of simplicity. My studies and experiments have set me something beyond good or evil. I see them fused as one or two facets of the same theme. Yet I have," he murmured, half to himself, "my low desires, my base instincts, and must at intervals satisfy them."

She did not understand what he meant, and as they neared the garden, which was full of noxious fumes of rotting flowers, her fears increased and when she saw the one light in the window of the Grange and he told her that was where her husband waited, she began to weep.

"Alas, poor creature," said Dr. Rowland, "I know not what power you have, but we must make the attempt. I am a physician, but I know when I meet cases beyond my skill."

"Is he ill?" sighed the lady. "Oh, ever since I was married to him I have feared disaster and disgrace."

"Perhaps even now you can avert it, madam. Yes, I think he is ill. He is like the ill-kept instruments among which he sits, all ajarred and out of tune, his mind full of delusions and his body full of pain. He moves as in a dark dream, and constantly sees wrestling phantoms."

They reached the house; the door was open and they entered without much sound and passed into the room where Dr. Rowland had left Sir William Notley.

They found the young man prostrate on a couch, still clasping the crucifix. His brow and upper lip glistened with sweat, and his coat was loosened at the throat.

At sight of his suffering all the lady's fears vanished. She came forward with the greatest confidence and kneeling by his side took his hand, so that both of them clasped the crucifix, and said:

"William, I have come to take you home. This is a desolate, and, I fear, an evil place."

He rose up then to a sitting posture and looked at her. Dr. Rowland brought the lantern from the window-place so that he might see her clearly. In that moment she was truly beautiful and her husband had not looked on real beauty since he had seen her last.

"Take her," said Dr. Rowland, "and ride away at once, not even staying to find a woman's saddle, but taking her up pillion behind you. You have done with the fantastic drama of Holcot Grange, and a reckless and despairing man stops at nothing to save himself, so begone."

Sir William gave his wife's hand a convulsive pressure and rose to his feet.

"Do not let go of her," said Dr. Rowland, still standing with the lantern held aloft. "Keep her close to you always. While she is with you you will not be conscious of those alluring forces, half-peril and half-delight, which have nearly destroyed you."

The Doctor bowed politely and the young couple left the room full of discarded, broken, musical instruments. He watched them go out into the quadrangle and pass through the great iron gates, she holding close on his arm, and looking lovingly up into his face, and presently while he listened he heard Sir William's horse bearing his wife away from Holcot Grange. And after that it was very silent.

Dr. Rowland was a little perplexed at his own sensations, but nothing could for long disturb one whose fancy had so many worlds in which to range. He was sorry that he would have to leave the oasthouse, but there was no choice.

He returned slowly under the mounting moon to his little dwelling and packed up all the implements of his experiments in readiness for an immediate departure. Nor would he, he knew, ever come to this part of the world again.

But Phœbe and Julia Roseingrave continued to live alone in the Dower House beyond the chestnut trees in the park.

THE END

SHORT STORIES

THE SCOURED SILK

This is a tale that might be told in many ways and from various points of view; it has to be gathered from here and there—a letter, a report, a diary, a casual reference; in its day the thing was more than a passing wonder, and it left a mark of abiding horror on the neighbourhood.

The house in which Mr. Orford lived has finally been destroyed, the mural tablet in St. Paul's, Covent Garden, may be sought for in vain by the curious, but little remains of the old piazza where the quiet scholar passed on his daily walks, the very records of what was once so real have become blurred, almost incoherent in their pleadings with things forgotten; but this thing happened to real people, in a real London, not so long ago that the generation had not spoken with those who remembered some of the actors in this terrible drama.

It is round the person of Humphrey Orford that this tale turns, as, at the time, all the mystery and horror centred; yet until his personality was brought thus tragically into fame, he had not been an object of much interest to many; he had, perhaps, a mild reputation for eccentricity, but this was founded merely on the fact that he refused to partake of the amusements of his neighbours, and showed a dislike for much company.

But this was excused on the ground of his scholarly predilections; he was known to be translating, in a leisurely fashion, as became a gentleman, Ariosto's great romance into English couplets, and to be writing essays on recondite subjects connected with grammar and language, which were not the less esteemed because they had never been published.

His most authentic portrait, taken in 1733 and intended for a frontispiece for the Ariosto when this should come to print, shows a slender man with reddish hair, rather severely clubbed, a brown coat, and a muslin cravat; he looks straight out of the picture, and the face is long, finely shaped, and refined, with eyebrows rather heavier than one would expect from such delicacy of feature.

When this picture was painted Mr. Orford was living near Covent Garden, close to the mansion once occupied by the famous Dr. Radcliffe, a straight-fronted, dark house of obvious gentility, with a little architrave portico over the door and a few steps leading up to it; a house with neat windows and a gloomy air, like every other residence in that street and most other streets of the same status in London.

And if there was nothing remarkable about Mr. Orford's dwelling place or person there was nothing, as far as his neighbours knew, remarkable about his history.

He came from a good Suffolk family, in which county he was believed to have considerable estates (though it was a known fact that he never visited them), and he had no relations, being the only child of an only child, and his parents dead; his father had purchased this town house in the reign of King William, when the neighbourhood was very fashionable, and up to it he had come, twenty years ago—nor had he left it since.

He had brought with him an ailing wife, a housekeeper, and a man-servant, and to the few families of his acquaintance near, who waited on him, he explained that he wished to give young Mrs. Orford, who was of a mopish disposition, the diversion of a few months in town.

But soon there was no longer this motive for remaining in London, for the wife, hardly seen by anyone, fell into a short illness and died—just a few weeks after her husband had brought her up from Suffolk. She was buried very simply in St. Paul's, and the mural tablet set up with a draped urn in marble, and just her name and the date, ran thus:

FLORA, WIFE OF HUMPHREY ORFORD, ESQ.,
OF THIS PARISH,
DIED NOVEMBER, 1713, AGED 27 YEARS.

Mr. Orford made no effort to leave the house; he remained, people thought, rather stunned by his loss, kept himself close in the house, and for a considerable time wore deep mourning.

But this was twenty years ago, and all had forgotten the shadowy figure of the young wife, whom so few had seen and whom no one had known anything about or been interested in, and all trace of her seemed to have passed out of the quiet, regular, and easy life of Mr. Orford, when an event that gave rise to some gossip caused the one-time existence of Flora Orford to be recalled and discussed among the curious. This event was none other than the sudden betrothal of Mr. Orford and the announcement of his almost immediate marriage.

The bride was one who had been a prattling child when the groom had first come to London: one old lady who was forever at her window watching the little humours of the street recollected and related how she had seen Flora Orford, alighting from the coach that had brought her from the country, turn to this child, who was gazing from the railing of the neighbouring house, and touch her bare curls lovingly and yet with a sad gesture.

And that was about the only time anyone ever did see Flora Orford, she so soon became ailing; and the next the inquisitive old lady saw of her was the slender brown coffin being carried through the dusk towards St. Paul's Church.

But that was twenty years ago, and here was the baby grown up into Miss Elisa Minden, a very personable young woman, soon to be the second Mrs. Humphrey Orford. Of course there was nothing very remarkable about the match; Elisa's father, Dr. Minden, had been Mr. Orford's best friend (as far as he could be said to have a best friend, or indeed any friend at all) for many a long year, both belonged to the same quiet set, both knew all about each other. Mr. Orford was not much above forty-five or so, an elegant, well-looking man, wealthy, with no vices and a calm, equable temper; while Miss Elisa, though pretty and well-mannered, had an insufficient dowry, no mother to fend for her, and the younger sisters to share her slender advantages. So what could anyone say save that the good doctor had done very well for his daughter, and that Mr. Orford had been fortunate enough to secure such a fresh, capable maiden for his wife?

It was said that the scholar intended giving up his bookish ways—that he even spoke of going abroad a while, to Italy, for preference; he was of course, anxious to see Italy, as all his life had been devoted to preparing the translation of an Italian classic.

The quiet betrothal was nearing its decorous conclusion when one day Mr. Orford took Miss Minden for a walk and brought her home round the piazza of Covent Garden, then took her across the cobbled street, past the stalls banked up with the first spring flowers (it was the end of March), under the portico built by the great Inigo Jones, and so into the church.

"I want to show you where my wife Flora lies buried," said Mr. Orford.

And that is really the beginning of the story.

Now, Miss Minden had been in this church every Sunday of her life and many weekdays, and had been used since a child to see that tablet to Flora Orford; but when she heard these words in the quiet voice of her lover and felt him draw her out of the sunlight into the darkness of the church, she experienced a great distaste that was almost fear.

It seemed to her both a curious and a disagreeable thing for him to do, and she slipped her arm out of his as she replied.

"Oh, please let us go home!" she said. "Father will be waiting for us, and your good Mrs. Boyd vexed if the tea is over-brewed."

"But first I must show this," he insisted, and took her arm again and led her down the church, past his seat, until they stood between his pew end and the marble tablet in the wall which was just a hand's space above their heads.

"That is to her memory," said Mr. Orford. "And you see there is nothing said as to her virtues."

Now, Elisa Minden knew absolutely nothing of her predecessor, and could not tell if these words were spoken in reverence or irony, so she said nothing but looked up rather timidly from under the shade of her Leghorn straw at the tall figure of her lover, who was staring sternly at the square of marble.

"And what have you to say to Flora Orford?" he asked sharply, looking down at her quickly.

"Why, sir, she was a stranger to me," replied Miss Minden. Mr. Orford pressed her arm.

"But to me she was a wife," he said. "She is buried under your feet. Quite close to where you are standing. Why, think of that, Lizzie, if she could stand up and put out her hand she could catch hold of your dress—she is as near as that!"

The words and his manner of saying them filled Miss Minden with shuddering terror, for she was a sensitive and fanciful girl, and it seemed to her a dreadful thing to be thus standing over the bones of the poor creature who had loved the man who was now to be her husband, and horrible to think that the handful of decay so near them had once clung to this man and loved him.

"Do not tremble, my dear girl," said Mr. Orford. "She is dead."

Tears were in Elisa Minden's eyes, and she answered coldly:

"Sir, how can you speak so?"

"She was a wicked woman," he replied, "a very wicked woman."

The girl could not reply as to that; this sudden disclosing of a painful secret abashed her simple mind.

"Need we talk of this?" she asked; then, under her breath—"Need we be married in this church, sir?"

"Of course," he answered shortly, "everything is arranged. Tomorrow week."

Miss Minden did not respond; hitherto she had been fond of the church, now it seemed spoilt for her—tarnished by the thought of Flora Orford.

Her companion seemed to divine what reflection lay behind her silence.

"You need not be afraid," he said rather harshly. "She is dead. Dead."

And he reached out the light cane he wore and tapped on the stone above his wife's grave, and slowly smiled as the sound rang hollow in the vaults beneath.

Then he allowed Elisa to draw him away, and they returned to Mr. Orford's comfortable house, where in the upper parlour Dr. Minden was awaiting them together with his sister and her son, a soldier cousin whom the quick perceptions of youthful friends had believed to be devoted to Elisa Minden. They made a pleasant little party with the red curtains drawn, and the fire burning up between the polished andirons and all the service for tea laid out with scones and Naples cake, and Mrs. Boyd coming to and fro with plates and dishes. And everyone was cheerful and friendly and glad to be indoors together, with a snowstorm coming up and people hurrying home with heads bent before a cutting wind.

But to Elisa's mind had come an unbidden thought:

"I do not like this house—it is where Flora Orford died."

And she wondered in which room, and also why this had never occurred to her before, and glanced rather thoughtfully at the fresh young face of the soldier cousin as he stood by the fire in his scarlet and white, with his glance on the flames.

But it was a cheerful party, and Elisa smiled and jested with the rest as she reserved the dishes at tea.

There is a miniature of her painted about this time, and one may see how she looked with her bright brown hair and bright brown eyes, rosy complexion, pretty nose and mouth, and her best gown of lavender blue tabinet with a lawn tucker and a lawn cap fastened under the chin with frilled lappets, showing how the big Leghorn hat with the velvet strings was put aside.

Mr. Orford also looked well tonight; he did not look his full age in the ruddy candle glow, the grey did not show in his abundant hair nor the lines in his fine face, but the elegance of his figure, the grace of his bearing, the richness of his simple clothes, were displayed to full advantage; Captain Hoare looked stiff and almost clumsy by contrast.

But now and then Elisa Minden's eyes would rest rather wistfully on the fresh face of this young man who had no dead wife in his life. And something was roused in her meek youth and passive innocence, and she wondered why she had so quietly accepted her father's arrangement of a marriage with this elderly scholar, and why Philip Hoare had let her do it. Her thoughts were quite vague and amounted to no more than a confused sense that something was wrong, but she lost her satisfaction in the tea-drinking and the pleasant company, and the warm room with the drawn curtains, and the bright fire, and rose up saying they must be returning, as there was a great store of mending she had promised to help her aunt with; but Mrs. Hoare would not help her out, but protested, laughing, that there was time enough for that, and the good doctor, who was in a fine humour and in no mood to go out into the bleak streets even as far as his own door, declared that now was the time they must be shown over the house.

"Do you know, Humphrey," he said, "you have often promised us this, but never done it, and, all the years that I have known you, I have never seen but this room and the dining-room below; and as to your own particular cabinet—"

"Well," said Mr. Orford, interrupting in a leisurely fashion, "no one has been in there, save Mrs. Boyd now and then, to announce a visitor."

"Oh, you scholars!" smiled the doctor. "A secretive tribe—and a fortunate one; why, in my poor room I have had three girls running to and fro!"

The soldier spoke, not so pleasantly as his uncle.

"What have you so mysterious, sir, in this same cabinet, that it must be so jealously guarded?" he asked.

"Why, nothing mysterious," smiled the scholar; "only my books, and papers, and pictures."

"You will show them to me?" asked Elisa Minden, and her lover gave graceful consent; there was further amiable talk, and then the whole party, guided by Mr. Orford holding a candle, made a tour of the house and looked over the fine rooms.

Mrs. Hoare took occasion to whisper to the bride-to-be that there were many alterations needed before the place was ready for a lady's use, and that it was time these were put in hand—why, the wedding was less than a fortnight off!

And Elisa Minden, who had not had a mother to advise her in these matters, suddenly felt that the house was dreary and old-fashioned, and an impossible place to live in; the very rooms that had so pleased her good father—a set of apartments for a lady—were to her the most hateful in the house, for they, her lover told her, had been furnished and prepared for Flora Orford, twenty years ago.

She was telling herself that when she was married she must at once go away and that the house must be altered before she could return to it, when the party came crowding to the threshold of the library or private cabinet, and Mr. Orford, holding the candle aloft, led them in. Then as this illumination was not sufficient, he went very quickly and lit the two candles on the mantelpiece.

It was a pleasant apartment, lined with books from floor to ceiling, old, valuable, and richly bound books, save only in the space above the chimney piece, which was occupied by a portrait of a lady and the panel behind the desk; this was situated in a strange position, in the farthest corner of the room fronting the wall, so that anyone seated there would be facing the door with the space of the room between; the desk was quite close to the wall, so that there was only just space for the chair at which the writer would sit, and to accommodate this there were no bookshelves behind it, but a smooth panel of wood on which hung a small picture; this was a rough, dark painting, and represented a man hanging on a gallows on a wild heath; it was a subject out of keeping with the luxurious room with its air of ease and learning, and while Mr. Orford was showing his first editions, his Elzevirs and Aldines, Elisa Minden was staring at this ugly little picture.

As she looked she was conscious of such a chill of horror and dismay as nearly caused her to shriek aloud. The room seemed to her to be full of an atmosphere of terror and evil beyond expression. Never had such a thing happened to her before; her visit to the tomb in the afternoon had been as nothing to this. She moved away, barely able to disguise an open panic. As she turned, she half-stumbled against a chair, caught at it, and noticed, hanging over the back, a skirt of peach-coloured silk. Elisa, not being mistress of herself, caught at this garment.

"Why, sir," cried she hysterically, "what is this?"

All turned to look at her; her tone, her obvious fright, were out of proportion to her discovery.

"Why, child," said Mrs. Hoare, "it is a silk petticoat, as all can see."

"A gift for you, my dear," said the cheerful doctor.

"A gift for me?" cried Elisa. "Why, this has been scoured, and turned, and mended, and patched a hundred times!"

And she held up the skirt, which had indeed become like tinder and seemed ready to drop to pieces.

The scholar now spoke.

"It belongs to Mrs. Boyd," he said quietly. "I suppose she had been in here to clean up, and has left some of her mending."

Now, two things about this speech made a strange impression on everyone; first, it was manifestly impossible that the good housekeeper would ever have owned such a garment as this, that was a lady's dress and such as would be worn for a ball; secondly, Mr. Orford had only a short while before declared that Mrs. Boyd only entered his room when he was in it, and then of a necessity and for a few minutes.

All had the same impression, that this was some garment belonging to his dead wife and as such cherished by him; all, that is, but Elisa, who had heard him call Flora Orford a wicked woman.

She put the silk down quickly (there was a needle sticking into it and a spool of cotton lying on the chair beneath) and looked up at the portrait above the mantelpiece.

"Is that Mrs. Orford?" she asked.

He gave her a queer look.

"Yes," he said.

In a strange silence all glanced up at the picture.

It showed a young woman in a white gown, holding a crystal heart that hung round her neck; she had dark hair and a pretty face; as Elisa looked at the pointed fingers holding the pretty toy, she thought of the tablet in St. Paul's Church and Mr. Orford's words—"She is so near to you that if she could stretch out her hand she could touch you," and without any remark about the portrait or the sitter, she advised her aunt that it was time to go home. So the four of them left, and Mr. Orford saw them out, standing framed in the warm light of the corridor and watching them disappear into the grey darkness of the street.

It was a little more than an hour afterwards when Elisa Minden came creeping down the stairway of her home and accosted her cousin, who was just leaving the house.

"Oh, Philip," said she, clasping her hands, "if your errand be not a very important one, I beg you to give me an hour of your time. I have been watching for you to go out, that I might follow and speak to you privately."

The young soldier looked at her keenly as she stood in the light of the hall lamp, and he saw that she was very agitated.

"Of course, Lizzie," he answered kindly, and led her into the little parlour off the hall where there was neither candles or fire, but leisure and quiet to talk.

Elisa, being a housekeeper, found a lamp and lit it, and apologised for the cold, but she would not return upstairs, she said, for Mrs. Hoare and the two girls and the doctor were all quiet in the great parlour, and she had no mind to disturb them.

"You are in trouble," said Captain Hoare quietly.

"Yes," replied she in a frightened way, "I want you to come with me now to Mr. Orford's house—I want to speak to his housekeeper."

"Why, what is this, Lizzie?"

She had no very good explanation; there was only the visit to the church that afternoon, her impression of horror in the cabinet, the discovery of the scoured silk.

"But I must know something of his first wife, Philip," she concluded. "I could never go on with it—if I did not—something has happened today—I hate that house, I almost hate—*him*."

"Why did you do it, Lizzie?" demanded the young soldier sternly. "This was a nice home-coming for me... a man who might be your father... a solitary... one who frightens you."

Miss Minden stared at her cousin; she did not know why she had done it; the whole thing seemed suddenly impossible.

"Please, you must come with me now," she said.

So overwrought was she that he had no heart to refuse her, and they took their warm cloaks from the hall and went out into the dark streets.

It was snowing now and the ground slippery under foot, and Elisa clung to her cousin's arm. She did not want to see Mr. Orford or his house ever again, and by the time they reached the doorstep she was in a tremble; but she rang the bell boldly.

It was Mrs. Boyd herself who came to the door; she began explaining that the master was shut up in his cabinet, but the soldier cut her short.

"Miss Minden wishes to see you," he said, "and I will wait in the hall till she is ready."

So Elisa followed the housekeeper down to her basement sitting-room; the man-servant was out, and the two maids were quickly dismissed to the kitchen.

Mrs. Boyd, a placid soul, near seventy-years, waited for the young lady to explain herself, and Elisa Minden, flushing and paling by turns, and feeling foolish and timid, put forth the object of her coming.

She wanted to hear the story of Flora Orford—there was no one else whom she could ask—and she thought that she had a right to know.

"And I suppose you have, my dear," said Mrs. Boyd, gazing into the fire, "though it is not a pretty story for you to hear—and I never thought I should be telling it to Mr. Orford's second wife!"

"Not his wife yet," said Miss Minden.

"There, there, you had better ask the master yourself," replied Mrs. Boyd placidly; "not but that he would be fierce at your speaking of it, for I do not think a mention of it has passed his lips, and it's twenty years ago and best forgotten, my dear."

"Tell it me and then I will forget," begged Miss Minden.

So then Mrs. Boyd, who was a quiet, harmless soul with no dislike to telling a tale (though no gossip, as events had proved, she having kept her tongue still on this matter for so long), told her story of Humphrey Orford's wife; it was told in very few words.

"She was the daughter of his gamekeeper, my dear, and he married her out of hand, just for her pretty face. But they were not very happy together that I could ever see; she was afraid of him and that made her cringe, and he hated that, and she shamed him with her ignorant ways. And then one day he found her with a lover, saving your presence, mistress, one of her own people, just a common man. And he was just like a creature possessed; he shut up the house and sent away all the servants but me, and brought his lady up to town, to this house here. And what passed

THE SCOURED SILK

between her and him no one will know, but she ever looked like one dying of terror. And then the doctor began to come, Dr. Thursby, it was, that is dead now, and then she died, and no one was able to see her even she was in her coffin, nor to send a flower. 'Tis likely she died of grief, poor, fond wretch. But, of course, she was a wicked woman, and there was nothing to do but pity the master."

And this was the story of Flora Orford.

"And the man?" asked Miss Minden, after a little.

"The man she loved, my dear? Well, Mr. Orford had him arrested as a thief for breaking into his house, he was wild, that fellow, with not the best of characters—well, he would not say why he was in the house, and Mr. Orford, being a Justice of the Peace, had some power, so he was just condemned as a common thief. And there are few to this day know the truth of the tale, for he kept his counsel to the last, and no one knew from *him* why he had been found in the Squire's house."

"What was his end?" asked Miss Minden in a still voice.

"Well, he was hanged," said Mrs. Boyd; "being caught red-handed, what could he hope for?"

"Then that is a picture of him in the cabinet!" cried Elisa, shivering for all the great fire; then she added desperately, "Tell me, did Flora Orford die in that cabinet?"

"Oh, no, my dear, but in a great room at the back of the house that has been shut up ever since."

"But the cabinet is horrible," said Elisa; "perhaps it is her portrait and that picture."

"I have hardly been in there," admitted Mrs. Boyd, "but the master lives there—he has always had his supper there, and he talks to that portrait my dear—'Flora, Flora' he says, 'how are you tonight?' and then he imitates her voice, answering."

Elisa Minden clapped her hand to her heart.

"Do not tell me these things or I shall think that you are hateful too, to have stayed in this dreadful house and endured them!"

Mrs. Boyd was surprised.

"Now, my dear, do not be put out," she protested.

"They were wicked people both of them and got their deserts, and it is an old story best forgotten; and as for the master, he has been just a good creature ever since we have been here, and he will not go talking to any picture when he has a sweet young wife to keep him company."

But Elisa Minden had risen and had her fingers on the handle of the door.

"One thing more," said she breathlessly; "that scoured silk—of a peach colour—"

"Why, has he got that still? Mrs. Orford wore it the night he found her with her sweetheart. I mind I was with her when she bought it—fine silk at forty shillings the yard. If I were you, my dear, I should burn that when I was mistress here."

But Miss Minden had run upstairs to the cold hall.

Her cousin was not there; she heard angry voices overhead and saw the two maid-servants affrighted on the stairs; a disturbance was unknown in this household.

While Elisa stood bewildered, a door banged, and Captain Hoare came down red in the face and fuming; he caught his cousin's arm and hurried her out of the house.

In an angry voice he told her of the unwarrantable behaviour of Mr. Orford, who had found him in the hall and called him "intruder" and "spy" without waiting for an explanation; the soldier had followed the scholar up to his cabinet and there had been an angry scene about nothing at all, as Captain Hoare said.

"Oh, Philip," broke out poor Elisa as they hastened through the cold darkness, "I can never, never marry him!"

And she told him the story of Flora Orford. The young man pressed her arm through the heavy cloak.

"And how came such a one to entangle thee?" he asked tenderly. "Nay, thou shalt not marry him."

They spoke no more, but Elisa, happy in the protecting and wholesome presence of her kinsman, sobbed with a sense of relief and gratitude. When they reached home they found they had been missed and there had to be explanations; Elisa said there was something that she had wished to say to Mrs. Boyd, and Philip told of Mr. Orford's rudeness and the quarrel that had followed.

The two elder people were disturbed and considered Elisa's behaviour strange, but her manifest agitation caused them to forbear pressing her for an explanation; nor was it any use addressing themselves to Philip, for he went out to his delayed meeting with companions at a coffee-house.

That night Elisa Minden went to bed feeling more emotion than she had ever done in her life; fear and disgust of the man whom hitherto she had placidly regarded as her future husband, and a yearning for the kindly presence of her childhood's companion united in the resolute words she whispered into her pillow during that bitter night.

"I can never marry him now!"

The next day it snowed heavily, yet a strange elation was in Elisa's heart as she descended to the warm parlour, bright from the fire and light from the glow of the snow without.

She was going to tell her father that she could not carry out her engagement with Mr. Orford, and that she did not want ever to go into his house again.

They were all gathered round the breakfast-table when Captain Hoare came in late (he had been out to get a newsletter) and brought the news that was the most unlooked for they could conceive, and that was soon to startle all London.

Mr. Orford had been found murdered in his cabinet.

These tidings, though broken as carefully as possible, threw the little household into the deepest consternation and agitation; there were shrieks, and cryings, and running to and fro.

Only Miss Minden, though of a ghastly colour, made no especial display of grief; she was thinking of Flora Orford.

When the doctor could get away from his agitated womenkind, he went with his nephew to the house of Mr. Orford.

The story of the murder was a mystery. The scholar had been found in his chair in front of his desk with one of his own bread-knives sticking through his shoulders; and there was nothing to throw any light as to how or through whom he had met his death.

The story, sifted from the mazed incoherency of Mrs. Boyd, the hysterics of the maids, the commentaries of the constables, and the chatter of the neighbours, ran thus:

At half-past nine the night before, Mrs. Boyd had sent one of the maids up with her master's supper; it was his whim to have it always thus, served on a tray in the cabinet. There had been wine and meat, bread and cheese, fruit and cakes—the usual plates and silver—among these the knife that had killed Mr. Orford.

When the servant left, the scholar had followed her to the door and locked it after her; this was also a common practice of his, a precaution against any possible interruption, for, he said, he did the best part of his work in the evening.

It was found next morning that his bed had not been slept in, and that the library door was still locked; as the alarmed Mrs. Boyd could get no answer to her knocks, the man-servant had sent for someone to force the lock, and Humphrey Orford had been found in his chair, leaning forward over his papers with the knife thrust up to the hilt between his shoulders; he must have died instantly, for there was no sign of any struggle, nor any disarrangement of his person or his papers. The first doctor to see him, a passer-by, attracted by the commotion about the house, said he must have been dead some hours—probably since the night before; the candles had all burnt down to the socket, and there were spillings of grease on the desk; the supper tray stood at the other end of the room, most of the food had been eaten, most of the wine drunk, the articles were all there in order excepting only the knife sticking between Mr. Orford's shoulder-blades.

When Captain Hoare had passed the house on his return from buying the newsletter he had seen the crowd and gone in and been able to say that he had been the last person to see the murdered man alive, as he had had his sharp encounter with Mr. Orford about ten o'clock, and he remembered seeing the supper things in the room. The scholar had heard him below, unlocked the door, and called out such impatient resentment of his presence that Philip had come angrily up the stairs and followed him into the cabinet;

a few angry words had passed, when Mr. Orford had practically pushed his visitor out, locking the door in his face and bidding him take Miss Minden home.

This threw no light at all on the murder; it only went to prove that at ten o'clock Mr. Orford had been alive in his cabinet.

Now here was the mystery; in the morning the door was still locked, *on the inside*, the window was, as it had been since early evening, shuttered and fastened across with an iron bar, *on the inside*, and, the room being on an upper floor, access would have been in any case almost impossible by the window which gave on to the smooth brickwork of the front of the house.

Neither was there any possible place in the room where anyone might be hidden—it was just the square lined with the shallow bookshelves, the two pictures (that sombre little one looking strange now above the bent back of the dead man), the desk, one or two chairs and side tables; there was not so much as a cupboard or bureau—not a hiding-place for a cat.

How, then, had the murderer entered and left the room?

Suicide, of course, was out of the question, owing to the nature of the wound—but murder seemed equally out of the question; Mr. Orford sat so close to the wall that the handle of the knife touched the panel behind him. For anyone to have stood between him and the wall would have been impossible; behind the back of his chair was not space enough to push a walking-stick.

How, then, had the blow been delivered with such deadly precision and force?

Not by anyone standing in front of Mr. Orford, first because he must have seen him and sprung up; and secondly, because, even had he been asleep with his head down, no one, not even a very tall man, could have leaned over the top of the desk and driven in the knife, for experiment was made, and it was found that no arm could possibly reach such a distance.

The only theory that remained was that Mr. Orford had been murdered in some other part of the room and afterwards dragged to his present position.

But this seemed more than unlikely, as it would have meant moving the desk, a heavy piece of furniture that did not look as if it had been touched, and also because there was a paper under the dead man's hand, a pen in his fingers, a splutter of ink where it had fallen, and a sentence unfinished. The thing remained a complete and horrid mystery, one that seized the imagination of men; the thing was the talk of all the coffee-houses and clubs.

The murder seemed absolutely motiveless, the dead man was not known to have an enemy in the world, yet robbery was out of the question, for nothing had been even touched.

The early tragedy was opened out. Mrs. Boyd told all she knew, which was just what she had told Elisa Minden—the affair was twenty years ago, and the gallows bird had no kith or kin left.

Elisa Minden fell into a desperate state of agitation, a swift change from her first stricken calm; she wanted Mr. Orford's house pulled down—the library and all its contents burnt; her own wedding-dress did she burn, in frenzied silence, and none dare stop her; she resisted her father's entreaties that she should go away directly after the inquest; she would stay on the spot, she said, until the mystery was solved.

Nothing would content her but a visit to Mr. Orford's cabinet; she was resolved, she said wildly, to come to the bottom of this mystery and in that room, which she had entered once and which had affected her so terribly, she believed she might find some clue.

The doctor thought it best to allow her to go; he and her cousin escorted her to the house that now no one passed without a shudder and into the chamber that all dreaded to enter.

Good Mrs. Boyd was sobbing behind them; the poor soul was quite mazed with this sudden and ghastly ending to her orderly life; she spoke all incoherently, explaining, excusing, and lamenting in a breath; yet through all her trouble she showed plainly and artlessly that she had had no affection for her master, and that it was custom and habit that had been wounded, not love.

Indeed, it seemed that there was no one who did love Humphrey Orford; the lawyers were already busy looking for a next-of-kin; it seemed likely that this property and the estates in Suffolk would go into Chancery.

"You should not go in, my dear, you should not go in," sobbed the old woman, catching at Miss Minden's black gown (she was in mourning for the murdered man) and yet peering with a fearful curiosity into the cabinet.

Elisa looked ill and distraught but also resolute.

"Tell me, Mrs. Boyd," said she, pausing on the threshold, "what became of the scoured silk?"

The startled housekeeper protested that she had never seen it again; and here was another touch of mystery—the old peach-coloured silk skirt that four persons had observed in Mr. Orford's cabinet the night of his murder, had completely disappeared.

"He must have burnt it," said Captain Hoare, and though it seemed unlikely that he could have consumed so many yards of stuff without leaving traces in the grate, still it was the only possible solution.

"I cannot think why he kept it so long," murmured Mrs. Boyd, "for it could have been no other than Mrs. Orford's best gown."

"A ghastly relic," remarked the young soldier grimly.

Elisa Minden went into the middle of the room and stared about her; nothing in the place was changed, nothing disordered; the desk had been moved round to allow of the scholar being carried away, his chair stood back, so that the long panel on which hung the picture of the gallows, was fuller exposed to view.

To Elisa's agitated imagination this portion of the wall sunk in the surrounding bookshelves, long and narrow, looked like the lid of a coffin.

"It is time that picture came down," she said; "it cannot interest anyone any longer."

"Lizzie, dear," suggested her father gently, "had you not better come away?—this is a sad and awful place."

"No," replied she. "I must find out about it—we must know."

And she turned about and stared at the portrait of Flora Orford.

"He hated her, Mrs. Boyd, did he not? And she must have died of fear—think of that!—died of fear, thinking all the while of that poor body on the gallows. He was a wicked man and whoever killed him must have done it to revenge Flora Orford."

"My dear," said the doctor hastily, "all that was twenty years ago, and the man was quite justified in what he did, though I cannot say I should have been so pleased with the match if I had known this story."

"How did we ever like him?" muttered Elisa Minden. "If I had entered this room before I should never have been promised to him—there is something terrible in it."

"And what else can you look for, my dear," snivelled Mrs. Boyd, "in a room where a man has been murdered."

"But it was like this before," replied Miss Minden; "it *frightened* me."

She looked round at her father and cousin, and her face quite distorted.

"There is something here now," she said, "something in this room."

They hastened towards her, thinking that her over-strained nerves had given way; but she took a step forward.

Shriek after shriek left her lips.

With a quivering finger she pointed before her at the long panel behind the desk.

At first they could not tell at what she pointed; then Captain Hoare saw the cause of her desperate terror.

It was a small portion of faded, peach-coloured silk showing above the ribbed line of the wainscot, protruding from the wall, like a garment of stuff shut in a door.

"She is in there!" cried Miss Minden. "In there!"

A certain frenzy fell on all of them; they were in a confusion, hardly knowing what they said or did. Only Captain Hoare kept some presence of mind and, going up to the panel, discerned a fine crack all round.

"I believe it is a door," he said, "and that explains how the murderer must have struck—from the wall."

He lifted the picture of the hanged man and found a small knob or button, which, as he expected, on being pressed sent the panel back into the wall, disclosing a secret chamber no larger than a cupboard.

And directly inside this hidden room that was dark to the sight and noisome to the nostrils, was the body of a woman, leaning against the inner wall with a white kerchief knotted tightly round her throat, showing how she had died; she wore the scoured silk skirt, the end of which had been shut in the panel, and an old ragged bodice of linen that was like a dirty parchment; her hair was grey and scanty, her face past any likeness to humanity, her body thin and dry.

The room, which was lit only by a window a few inches square looking onto the garden, was furnished with a filthy bed of rags and a stool with a few tattered clothes; a basket of broken bits was on the floor.

Elisa Minden crept closer.

"It is Flora Orford," she said, speaking like one in a dream.

They brought the poor body down into the room, and then it was clear that this faded and terrible creature had a likeness to the pictured girl who smiled from the canvas over the mantelpiece.

And another thing was clear and, for a moment, they did not dare speak to each other.

For twenty years this woman had endured her punishment in the wall chamber in that library that no one but her husband entered; for twenty years he had kept her there, behind the picture of her lover, feeding her on scraps, letting her out only when the household was abed, amusing himself with her torture—she mending the scoured silk she had worn for twenty years, sitting there, cramped in the almost complete dark, a few feet from where he wrote his elegant poetry.

"Of course she was crazy," said Captain Hoare at length, "but why did she never cry out?"

"For a good reason," whispered Dr. Minden, when he had signed to Mrs. Boyd to take his fainting daughter away. "He saw to that—*she has got no tongue.*"

The coffin bearing the nameplate "*Flora Orford*" was exhumed, and found to contain only lead; it was substituted by another containing the wasted body of a woman who died by her own hand twenty years after the date on the mural tablet to her memory.

Why or how this creature, certainly become idiotic and dominated entirely by the man who kept her prisoner, had suddenly found the resolution and skill to slay her tyrant and afterwards take her own life (a thing she might have done any time before) was a question never solved.

It was supposed that he had formed the hideous scheme to complete his revenge by leaving her in the wall to die of starvation while he left with his new bride for abroad, and that she knew this and had forestalled him; or else that her poor, lunatic brain had been roused by the sound of a woman's voice as she handled the scoured silk which the captive was allowed to creep out and mend when the library door was locked. But over these matters and the details of her twenty years' suffering, it is but decent to be silent.

Lizzie Minden married her cousin, but not at St. Paul's, Covent Garden. Nor did they ever return to the neighbourhood of Humphrey Orford's house.

DARK ANN

Nothing could have been more neutral, more dull; the scene was the lecture hall of one of our most learned societies, as austere and grim a place as the cold mind and lifeless taste of Science could conceive, or anyhow did conceive and execute in the days when this hall, and many others, was built.

A lecture was in progress.

A man as austere, as grim as the hall, but in the same way rather grand and imposing, was in the rostrum, talking about hygiene and sanitation.

Like the hall, like the society, he seemed, in his disdain of any concession to the lighter graces, dreary and forbidding, ageless, featureless, drab.

I wondered why I had come; Minnie Levine had brought me; she was one of those women who try, and quite successfully, to make good works fashionable.

This had brought her into the chill and lofty circle where Sir William Torrance moved, and, somehow, to this lecture.

Not altogether purposelessly, for afterwards we were to take the great man back to Minnie's reception and introduce him to a number of other earnest and charming workers in the cause of health and happiness for others.

Minnie had said a great deal about the personality of the lecturer, but to me he seemed to have no personality; he was part of the remote classic decorations of that depressing room, something almost dehumanised.

Yet, as I studied the man (for there was nothing else to do since I could not concentrate on the matter of his speech), I discovered that he was not by any means unattractive, though subdued to the drab dignity of his surroundings, eclipsed by the sombre correctness of his orthodox clothes, those dull blacks, greys and icy white linen.

He was not so old though his hair was ash coloured, his face haggard, not so old, I was sure, perhaps forty-eight, fifty. Handsome features, aquiline, dark, with a narrow high nose and full lips, bluish eyes, cold and clever, a figure that would have been graceful enough if he had not so carefully refrained from any movement, any gesture, if he had not held himself with such monotonous stateliness.

The lecture was over; I thought I caught Minnie's sigh of relief.

I, too, was glad to leave, though it was a cruel winter's day without, colourless, biting, grim.

We waited for the lecturer; he carefully and gravely answered the earnest questioners who came timidly up to the platform, then waited for us, methodically rolling up his charts of "Drainage Systems for Country Houses" that he had been showing us.

He was presented to me and I felt further depressed by his lifeless courtesy; perhaps he had heard of me as a foolish trifler in dreams and visions, a writer of stories fantastical and strange; I felt uncomfortable thinking how he must despise me; of course I didn't believe he had any right to despise me, yet, unreasonably it made me wince to realise that he probably did, he had so much weight about him, an air of being unassailable.

He hadn't much to say as we went home in Minnie's car; I believe he was wondering why he had consented to come. I've often seen that surprised resentment lurking in the eyes of Minnie's celebrated guests.

What he did say was heavy and wise, fragments of his lecture.

"Instructive but not amusing," whispered Minnie, "but rather a dear, don't you think?"

"No, I really don't. He knows too much—he's quite dried up."

"But so good-looking," insisted Minnie. "And not married—"

"A lucky escape for some woman"—the obvious gibe came sincerely to my lips. "Think of being married to a treatise on Sanitation—"

"Oh, he's much more than that," said Minnie earnestly, "a really *great* doctor, you know."

I did know, but I was quite vague as to his actual achievements; one generally is vague as to the achievements of those outside one's own world.

I noticed him once or twice, impassive, bored, grave, among the guests; I was surprised not to see the familiar gesture of the hand to the watch, the murmur of "an appointment" which is such a man's usual escape from a crowd of women.

But he stayed.

When tea was over and dancing had begun, he, alone for a moment, looked round as if searching for someone.

He caught my eye and came so directly over to me that my companion rose at once and wandered off.

Sir William took the vacant chair; I was more overwhelmed than flattered.

"You must have been very bored this afternoon," he said seriously.

I replied that I rather made a point of never being bored, but that I'd been depressed—and understood very little; I paid him the compliment of not trying to "play up" to him.

"Of course you were. You write, don't you?"

"Only a little. As an amateur."

"I've read them. *Phantasmagoria*."

This was amazing.

"Yes, they're phantasmagoria—don't you love the word? But strange you should bother with them, Sir William."

"Do you think so?"

"Well—I shouldn't have thought you'd have much time for that kind of thing."

He looked at me, wistfully, I thought.

"Yet I could tell you something."

And then he was silent, as if I had discouraged him; he seemed so remote from the scene, the warm, shaded room, the dancers, the hot-house flowers, that he made me too feel detached.

We were sitting a little apart in one of Minnie's famous alcoves lit by a painted alabaster lamp; we were left alone, because all the others were enjoying themselves.

Minnie glanced at me and nodded cheerfully; I think that she was rather glad to have the great man taken off her hands.

As for him, I really think he was as unconscious of his surroundings now as he had been during his lecture, he never asked if I danced, he never seemed to notice that anyone was dancing.

He spoke again, almost in a challenging tone.

"Do I seem to you very alien to all that?" he asked.

I was at a loss as to what thought he was finishing with this sentence, and so I said:

"All—what?"

He hesitated.

"Romance is perhaps the word."

Even to me that word was rather profaned.

"Oh, Romance—"

"I use it," said Sir William stiffly, "in the purest sense. It has of course been cheapened by our lesser writers. Like several other beautiful words—love, lovely, and others. They become *clichés*, slick, disgusting. Think, however, what Romance would mean to a lonely man who never saw a newspaper or heard a gossip and never read a book that was less than two hundred years old."

I agreed that everything was overdone.

"Nothing fresh is left," I lamented, "every story has been told and staled."

Sir William corrected me.

"You should know better. Told, but not staled. What of a kiss, the rose's scent? You've been kissed before, if you're lucky; you've smelt a rose before, if you've any sense—yet you are just as eager for the present kiss, the present rose.

"And with Romance. It is always the same Romance, of course, but only a fool seeks for novelty."

He spoke abstractedly, dryly, and his words, so at variance with his manner, surprised me a great deal.

"It is quite true," I said, "but I hardly thought you would know as much, Sir William."

"Why?"

I did not know how to explain to him how remote, how stern, how impressive and cold he seemed.

"You're too wise," I said, "you know too much to know that."

"Exactly. 'With all thy wisdom get understanding,' eh? Yes, I know too much, and none of it much use. But I know that too. A materialist may have his glimpses into spiritual matters."

"Not if he's really a materialist, Sir William."

He ignored that.

"I came here to speak to you," he said in a coldly impersonal tone, "because of some things of yours I've read. I thought I'd like to tell you something that happened to me, perhaps get you to write it down as a sort of record. One ages, memory weakens. I always fear that what is so vivid today tomorrow may be dim. That is," he added with perfunctory politeness, "if it interests you."

I said with truth that it did interest me. Of course.

"That's good of you. And then, on my death—I am considerably your senior—you might publish the story, as—a lesson to other people."

He looked at his watch (the familiar gesture at last!) and excused himself in conventional tones.

Another time perhaps he might tell me the story? Or, no, there wasn't a story. I hoped he wouldn't forget, but thought he would.

Three days later he rang up to ask for an appointment; I begged him to come that afternoon; I should be alone.

He came; immaculate, stately, unsmiling, very impressive.

And, after an apology for tea, he began speaking, looking into the fire the while just as if I wasn't there; I saw at once that he was intensely lonely and that it was an immense joy and relief for him to speak, which he did carefully and without a trace of emotion, in a concise, stately language.

"It's twenty years ago, 1905, exactly twenty years, in the winter. I was very hard-working, very absorbed and very successful for a youngster. I had no ties and a little money of my own, I'd taken all the degrees and honours I could take, and I'd just finished a rather stiff German course in Munich—physical chemistry—and I was rather worn out.

"I had not begun to practise and I decided to rest before I did so.

"I recognised in myself those dangerous symptoms of fatigue, lack of interest in everything and a nervous distrust of my powers. And by nature I was fairly confident, even, I daresay, arrogant.

"While I was still in Munich a cousin I had almost forgotten, died and left me a house and furniture.

"Not of much value and in a very out-of-the-way place.

"I thought the bequest queer and paid no attention to it; of course I was rather pleased, but I decided to sell.

"I meant to live in London and I had not the least intention of an early marriage, nor indeed of any marriage at all.

"I was nearly thirty and sufficiently resolute and self-contained.

"When I returned to London and consulted my lawyers about the sale of the house, which was called 'Stranger's End,' they advised that I should see it first and check the inventories of the contents.

"They said that there were some curious old pieces there I might care to keep; I did not think this likely, as I had no interest in such things, but I thought I would go to see the house.

"I was too tired for pleasure or amusement; one can be, you know.

"The thought of this lonely, quiet house attracted me; it was near Christmas and I dreaded the so-called festivities, the invitations of friends, the upset to routine.

"I went to 'Stranger's End' and my first impression justified my lawyers' warning; it was not a very saleable property.

"The house stood one end of a lonely Derbyshire valley, on the site of one much older that had been burnt down.

"The style was classic—Palladian, purplish brick, white pilasters, hard, square, ugly, more like Kent than Wren.

"The garden had been very formal, with *broderie* beds, but was neglected, the stucco summer-houses, statues and fountains being in a dilapidated condition, and the parterres a tangle of wild growth.

"The situation was lonely in the extreme, really isolated; the railway had missed the valley and there was no passable motor road near; the approaches to 'Stranger's End' were mean tracks across moor and mountain."

Sir William Torrance was silent here; he seemed to sink into deep abstraction, as he stared into the fire.

And I, too, could see what he was seeing, that solitary, pretentious, ugly and neglected mansion in the Derbyshire dales.

"It sounds haunted," I suggested.

He roused himself.

"No, it wasn't. I never heard the least suggestion of that. There was no story about the place at all. It had come to my cousin through his father's people; our connection was through the female side, and they had been quiet, prosperous folk who hadn't for a hundred years lived much at 'Stranger's End.' But my cousin, an eccentric sort of man, had taken a liking to the place."

"Why did he leave it to you?"

"I don't know. We had been slightly friendly as boys, but he was queer. We went such different ways. He was a little older than

I. And died rather tragically, through an accident. Well, there was the place. I liked it.

"Really relished the isolation; I was terrified of a breakdown, of losing my capacity, my zest for work; I thought—whatever I do, I'll get fit.

"That was a very severe winter, at least in Derbyshire; the fells and dales were covered with snow, and all that cracked stucco frippery in the garden, those sham deities of the eighteenth century, were outlined in white and masked in ice.

"I had no personal servant in those days; the caretaker, an old man, and his widowed daughter looked after me; they were rather a dour couple but efficient enough and seemed attached to 'Stranger's End,' for they asked if I would 'speak for them' to my purchaser who did not yet exist.

"The house was furnished exactly as you would expect it to be, panelled walls, heavy walnut furniture, indigo blue green tapestry, gilt wood mirrors, and pictures of the schools of Van Dyck and Kneller.

"It was a large house, much larger than you would think from that stern facade, and I was there a while before I knew all the rooms.

"I enjoyed, with a sense of irony, the grandeur of the state bedroom which probably had chiefly been used for the 'lying in state' of defunct owners.

"The four-poster was adorned by dusky plumes and curtains stiff with needlework, rotting at the cracks and faded a peculiar dove-like colour."

Sir William spoke with a lingering relish curious to hear.

"Strange," I thought, "that he should remember all these details, strange, too, that this is the man who gave that drab lecture in that drab hall."

He seemed to want no encouragement nor comment from me, and continued in his level, pleasant tones that were so virile and powerful even when muted as they were now.

"I found, during those first few days, several odd pieces in the house. Of course I had nothing to do but look for them.

"It was ferociously cold and snowed steadily; all prospect from the windows even was blotted out.

"Among other things I found a little box of blue velvet sewn with a very intricate design in seed pearl and embroidered in gold thread—'Made by mee, Darke Ann.' Impossible to describe how that fascinated me!

"An empty, trifling sort of box, rather worn, odorous of some aromatic—musk or tonquin.

"Made by 'Darke Ann'!

"Why should she so describe herself, in that formal age to which she belonged?

"There was no date, but I thought the thing went back to the time of my grandmother.

"It was because, perhaps, my brain was so exhausted, because I was so studiously keeping it free from all serious matter, that this absurd detail so obsessed me; I had never had any imagination nor cared for fanciful things, I'd worked too hard.

"But now, when my mind was empty this seized on it— 'Darke Ann.'

"I had no difficulty in visualising her; I could see her moving about the house, bending over that box, looking out of the windows on to the snow."

"The house, then, was haunted after all," I suggested.

Sir William denied this earnestly.

"No. I have been trying to convey to you that it was not.

"Nothing of the kind. It was merely that I, shut up alone in this queer (to me) house in this great solitude, was able to picture, very clearly, this creature of my fancy.

"Purely of my fancy:

"You know how the snow will give one that enclosed feeling, shut in alone, remote, softly imprisoned.

"So few people came to the house, and those few I never saw.

"Then one night—it could not have been long before Christmas, of which festival I took no account—I went up to my room holding a lamp—there was no other means of lighting in the old house—and glancing at the bed I saw there—"

He paused, and when he continued I had the strangest sensation, for this man, so dry, so austere, so conventionally clothed, whom I had heard lecturing on "Sanitation," whose reputation was so lofty, whose life and career were well known to have been so dry, cold and laborious, spoke like a poet making an embroidery of beautiful words.

"A woman," he went on with infinite tenderness. "She lay lightly to one side with her arms crossed, so that the delicate fingers rested on her rounded elbows, but so lightly! She wore a plain robe and a cap with a crimped edge, tied under her chin; tucked into her breast was a posy of flowers, winter flowers, aconite, I think. She was so fine, so airy that she did not press the bed at all, but rested there, as a little bird might rest on a water flower without rippling the pool.

"She smiled; her face was soft and dimpled, her eyes closed, yet not so completely that a streak of azure did not show beneath the fragile lids; her lips were full, but pale—the whole colour of her pearl and mist, merged into the faded tarnish of the bed."

Sir William, who had been gazing into the fire, suddenly looked at me.

"Not a ghost," he said. "I knew she was not there. I knew the bed was empty. Hallucination is perhaps the word. I had been over-working. Mind and nerves were strained.

"I told myself that she was not there, and I seated myself with my needless lamp beside the bed and looked at her; I say, needless lamp, for when I had extinguished it, I saw her in the dark as easily, as precisely.

"Then the window must rattle at the pane and make me look round with a start, and when I looked back again she was gone.

"The next day I examined my casket of blue velvet with even greater tenderness, and chancing to pull at a little odd thread, ripped the stuff, so old and perished it was, so that there was an ugly slit across the lid.

"I was looking at this in much chagrin when my caretaker entered.

"'Who would this be?' I asked, as lightly as I could. 'Darke Ann?'

"'That would be Lady Ann Marly, sir,' he answered sullenly. 'There's her portrait upstairs.'

"'Where?' I was startled.

"'In the attics. I don't think you've been up to the attics, sir.'

"I went; that bitter, windy day I went up to the attics of 'Stranger's End.' The snow had ceased and I could see the valley white from end to end, and the hills, sombre against a sky like a grey goose's breast.

"There was the portrait, standing with others amid dusty lumber, cobwebs and decay.

"It was she, of course, Dark Ann, but as I turned the picture round I was shocked.

"She was so much further away than I had thought.

"A hundred years, I had guessed, but the costume was that of the first Charles, a tight gown of grey satin, monstrous pearls at throat and ears, a confusion of jet black ringlets and the face that I had seen in my—hallucination.

"It was a fine painting by that sterling artist, Janssens van Ceulen, and I wondered why it had been banished to that sad obscurity.

"On the black background was painted '*The Lady Ann Marly, aetat. 25, "Darke Ann."*'

"Dark she was, as a gipsy, as a Spaniard, in eyes and hair, yet pure and clear in her complexion as a lily, as a rose.

"I had the picture taken downstairs and hung in the room where I usually sat. The man, old Doveton, knew nothing of the portrait, or of the Lady Ann Marly, only what I could see for myself, the names on canvas and casket, but he told me that the Marlys were buried in Baswell Church and probably this 'black Madam' amongst them, and also that there was an antique shop in the same town where I could get my casket repaired.

"I will not bother you," said Sir William at this part of his extraordinary narrative, "with any of my feelings, moods, or states of mind. I will merely tell you the facts.

"The first day it was fit to leave the house (for the snow had fallen again in great abundance), I went down across the valley to Baswell, a town so small, so old, so grim and silent, that it seemed to me like a thing imagined, not seen.

"The church, heavy, mutilated, dark, squatted on a little slope and was flanked by tombs so gaunt, monstrous, ponderous and grim as to seem a very army of death; the snow touched them here and there with a ghastly white, and the ivy on the tower was a green darker than black against that pallid winter sky.

"Inside, the place was musty, dull, crowded with tombs, knights, priests, ladies, children in busts and effigies—so much dust on everything!

"As if it had risen from the vaults below to choke the holy air!

"The pale dimness of the faint December light struggled through panes of old, dingy glass in withered reds and blues, only to be blocked by melancholy pillars and frowning arches.

"I found her tomb; a gigantic rococo urn draped with a fringed cloth with boastful letters setting forth her prides and virtues, and a Latin epigram, florid and luscious, punning on her name of 'Dark Ann' and the eternal Darkness that had swallowed her loveliness.

"She had died, unmarried, 'of a sudden feaver' in her 25th year, 1648.

"The year the portrait was painted.

"I had the casket in my pocket and I set out to find the antique shop.

"There was only one, in a side street, in a house as old, as sad, as grim as the church, with a tiny window, crowded by melancholy lumber, the broken toys and faded vanities of the dead.

"Clocks that had stopped for ever, rusty vessels from which no one would drink again, queer necklaces no woman would ever again clasp round her throat, snapped swords and chipped tea cups—oh, a very medley of pathetic rubbish!

"I pulled the bell, for the door was locked, and was opened immediately by a woman who stood smiling and asking me in out of the uncharitable afternoon.

"It was Dark Ann—or, as my common sense assured me, a creature exactly like her.

"'What is your name?' I asked stupidly.

"'Ann Marly,' she replied in the sweetest accents.

"'Why, I've just been looking at your tomb.'

"She smiled, not, though, surprised.

"'I believe there is such a name in the church—many of them, indeed. The Marlys were great people round about here. And yet we have been long away and only just returned.'

"As she spoke she held the door for me and I entered the low, dusky shop, which was piled with lumber and lit by only a twilight greyness.

"'Long away?' I echoed.

"'Yes, a long time,' she smiled. 'And, please what did you want?'

"In a delicious amaze I handed her the casket; she looked at it and sighed.

"'You want that mended?'

"'Yes, please—she was called Dark Ann and that should be your name too, you know.'

"She did not answer this, but said gravely that the box could be mended—she herself would do the exquisite stitching.

"I could look at nothing but the lady—I must use this word; neither woman nor girl will express this creature.

"She wore a dark dress that might have been of any period, low in the neck, and the clouds of her dark ringlets were lightly confined by a comb I could not see.

"She asked me into an old room at the back of the shop, and there she gave me tea in shallow yellow cups.

"The whole place was old, she said—the high-backed cane chairs in which we sat, the boards beneath our feet, the beams above our heads, the dark pictures of carnations and gillyflowers in gilt bronze frames, the sea green glass mirror in red tortoiseshell, all these things were old.

"She and her grandfather had opened the little shop only lately, and only, it seemed, because they wanted to come back to Baswell; she told me nothing more of herself; nor did I speak of myself.

"I could not think of her as another than the Dark Ann of the portrait, the casket, the tomb; I did not wish to think of her as another; hallucination and reality blended in one.

"I went over every day to see her; it was understood we were lovers, that we should marry and live at 'Stranger's End' all our lives.

"Understood but not spoken of—

"Once I brought her up to the ugly, queer house that now I no longer had any intention of selling.

"I had found an old pair of tiny gauntlets in a chest, much worn, fringed with gold; she slipped them on, and they fitted to the very creases.

"Enough of this.

"As you know, one can't describe a rapture—sometimes, when I stood near her, there was a sense of radiance, well—

"With every year it becomes more difficult to recall, sometimes I forget it altogether, and yet I know it was there, it actually happened—that time of ecstasy."

He was silent for a little, and in my quiet room I could see the glittering evanescent gleams of a vision that would not wholly vanish through all the prosaic years.

"And I suppose," I said, "that you forgot your work and your ambitions."

He looked at me sharply.

"That was exactly what happened. I remembered nothing, I lived in the moment, I hardly thought even of the future, though that was to be spent with her. I lived in that queer, ugly house in that lonely valley, and I went to and fro that grim, silent little town, accompanied by snow, wind and clouds, to sit in the little dim parlour behind the huddled shop and drink tea with Ann Marly out of those flat yellow cups, beneath the old beams, the old pictures, lit by a clear fire that glittered on the smooth surface of bluish tiles with puce-coloured landscapes, and the mellow radiance of wax candles in heavy plated sticks that showed the red copper through where they were worn."

"You remember it all very distinctly, Sir William."

"Even the threads in her dress—where the sleeve was sewn to the bodice—a little lighter than the silk.

"I said I would keep to the facts," he sighed. "So let all that go. One day I received a telegram.

"I read it as if it had been in an unknown language at first.

"When I came to understand it, I remembered who I was, where I was, what I had been and hoped to be, what was expected of me.

"It was from a friend, a man I greatly admired and respected, a really eminent, brilliant doctor—

"It was a long telegram.

"At that time Medicine was beginning to be very interested in Encephalitis Lethargica and a Swiss doctor claimed to have found a—what you would call a cure. Would I go, with three other men and investigate, report, and if need be, learn the treatment?

"I was excited, alert; I wired back an acceptance; in twenty-four hours I was in London.

"I had been tremendously interested in this disease, so rare, deadly and horrible, with its terrible sequel of dementia praecox, change of character and loss of memory, and I was again the careful, keen man of science, trained to test, to doubt, to explore—

"We were in the train for Geneva before I thought of Dark Ann.

"I wired her from the first stop; I didn't really know her address, I had never noticed the name of the shop or the street, but I put 'Miss Ann Marly, Baswell, Derby'; the place was so small I had no doubt it would find her; I wrote from Geneva, I said I was coming back.

"I wrote and wired often enough during three weeks.

"But she never sent me any message.

"I blamed myself; my flight had been atrocious, I could not explain it to myself, it was extraordinary, incredible. I had started off like a man wakened from a dream!

"She was offended, angry. I thought it reasonable that she should be, I thought of her always as waiting for me.

"It was a month before I got back—the Swiss doctor's work was interesting, but there was nothing in it, really.

"I returned to Derbyshire.

"It was still cold, grey, iron-like in earth and sky.

"'Why on earth is this house called "Stranger's End"?' I asked old Doveton.

"'I don't know, sir. But it was a fancy in those old days, I think.'

"I went to Baswell.

"And this is pretty well the end of my story," said Sir William ironically.

"She was dead?"

"I could not find the shop. In the street where I could have sworn it was, stood an old empty house; the neighbours said it had been empty a long time, they remembered no antique shop, no Ann Marly—they were vague, stupid, unfriendly.

"I ransacked the town; she, her grandfather, the shop with that delicious parlour had utterly disappeared.

"I went to the post office and they showed me the last of my little heap of letters; the others had travelled back to Switzerland through the dead letter office and must now be waiting for me at my London address.

"'There's a name like this in the church,' said the postmaster sullenly, looking at me queerly, 'on a tomb. I've never heard of another here.'

"I brought Doveton in to Baswell and made him point out the shop he had recommended for the repair of the velvet box.

"He showed me a dingy furniture shop in the High Street where they did upholstering.

"I asked him if he remembered the lady who had come to 'Stranger's End.'

"And the sulky fellow said that he did not, which may have been true, for I brought her and took her away myself and I do not think she met either of the servants."

I knew that he had never found her; the room seemed full of a miasma of regret, of remorse, of yearning.

"So you went back to your work," I said tentatively, for I was not sure of his control.

"Yes, I did. I sold the house and all the contents." He looked at me wildly. "I burnt the portrait, I could not endure it. I sold the house to the neighbouring lord who wanted the ground for his shooting—it was just in his way, that old garden, that old ugly house. He destroyed both. I wouldn't have sold to anyone who had not promised to destroy."

He looked withered, shrunk.

"I have the little blue box, so neatly mended, full of dead aconites, like she held against her breast—"

"You're confusing the vision and the reality," I said; "that—hallucination must have been the first Ann—after death, I rather think."

"After death," repeated Sir William.

"You've done good work," I reminded him, "devoted yourself to real, fine, man's work—she would have spoilt you for that, perhaps."

He said drearily:

"Yes, I've had my work. And nothing else."

"Well, fame, applause, gratitude, money, honours."

"Oh, those," he looked at me vaguely, "but I never had another dream. Not one. Now if that telegram hadn't come—"

He paused and I finished for him:

"It broke the spell, you mean. It restored you to your normal self—it made you return to your normal life."

"Exactly." He was now composed, austere, even ironic again. "I would give all I've ever gained since to have that moment again, to have that choice—the dream or the bread and water. And at the moment I didn't know it was a choice."

"You wish you hadn't gone?"

He rose.

"Do I wish I hadn't gone! Haven't I told you the story as a warning? That was the only real thing that ever happened to me."

He turned to the door.

"But Ann, Ann Marly?" I asked. "What of her? Why did she disappear?"

"Why did she come, you mean," he answered dryly. "I lost her, because I forgot how to dream."

"You mean—she didn't really exist?" I felt a pang of fear.

Sir William Torrance smiled.

"I'm due the other end of London at six—I've talked you to death. Good-bye."

His manner was correct, lifeless again; I knew from the papers that he was lecturing on "Bacteriology in Food" at some institute.

I let him go, there was nothing to be said.

HURRY! HURRY!

Eügen Töllong offered money in vain; none of the boatmen would row him across the lake; the ice was breaking and the dark water choked by cracking floes.

He was desperate enough to risk an accident.

"A matter of life or death?" they asked.

Töllong smiled behind his high fur collar; quick riding through the wind had flayed his cheeks a burning red; his eyes, under the heavy cloth cap, showed a hard, bright blue that seemed as unnaturally vivid as coloured glass.

"Certainly it is a matter of life and death—my motto, since I began my journey, has been—hurry!"

"Very well, then, if you go a little further up the lake, where the ice is firmer, you can hire a sledge, and if you care to drive it yourself; with your own horse—"

Töllong turned, waiting to hear no more, and rode along the edge of the vast lake that stretched between him and the capital, the objective of his swift journey; to have gone round by the road would have meant a delay that he could not afford.

The landscape was bare as a bleached bone; even the distant line of pines on the further shore appeared frozen in stark immobility; ash-grey geese flew across a cold, pallid sky; in subdued, menacing tumult the water strove against the ice; as he hastened, Töllong heard this crack, saw, in the deep splits, the dark, bitter wavelets.

HURRY! HURRY!

He procured a sledge by paying the value of it in advance; the people at the lonely post house were amazed at his lavishness, at his recklessness.

"The ice will scarcely bear—this must be very important business!"

"I have but one word in my ears and that is—'hurry!'" replied Töllong; he reflected that he was making himself conspicuous, that these inquisitive people would remember him—afterwards.

But that would not matter; it was not as if he had reckoned on escape; still it was a pity that the affair had been left so late and that the spring had chanced so early this year.

He leaped into the sledge to which his stout, fresh horse had been harnessed, placed his case, the only luggage he carried, beside him, drew closely round his limbs the reindeer rugs and started off across the ice which there lay smooth enough; now and then he heard a crack beneath him which startled the horse, and urged the frightened beast on as fiercely as if the wolves were behind; as he neared the further shore he felt the heave of the ice crust beneath him; it was breaking. Töllong stood up, loosened the reins, yelled at the plunging horse, trying to guide him to the block of ice ahead—the foreshore was so close, failure seemed impossible, he could discern a wooden house at the verge of the black wood, a man, a boat among the frozen reeds.

Töllong's horse missed the ice floe, and plunged into the lake, dragging the sledge after him; Töllong struggled in the sharp cold water, was sucked under and lost his senses; the hideous sensation of swimming in blackness gave way to one of drowsy warmth; he felt something hot in his mouth and sat up suddenly, spilling the liquid on his chest. "Hurry!" he muttered, making an effort to rise; but he was held back and answered by a laugh.

"Yes—hurry, indeed. Fool's haste!—and fool's luck too—you're all right."

Töllong lay quiet as his senses, his memories flowed back to him; he was on a rough bed by a huge stove that warmed a plain wooden room; before this his own clothes and those of another were drying; on the top of it, coffee was heating and a pan of food cooking; Töllong stretched and looked round for the man who had spoken.

"You rescued me?" he asked, stupidly.

"Well, I had to pull you out of the lake—why did they let you attempt the crossing?"

"I insisted—my business is very important."

Töllong sat up; he was covered in rugs and skins and wore a shirt not his own; he felt foolish and vexed as he tried to express to his rescuer some gratitude, some appreciation.

This young man was about his own age, of a fine physique; he had changed into a linen shirt, that hung open carelessly on his broad white chest, and blue cloth breeches; his wide, comely face expressed great vitality and vivacity; he was obviously full of gaiety and daring; his thick fair hair, roughly dried, hung on to his shoulders, giving him an uncouth appearance; but for all that, Töllong noted at once his elegance and distinction.

"You are not a farmer or a peasant," he said—"who are you?"

The other answered this blunt question candidly.

"I am an officer in the garrison in Stockholm—and I came out here for a little duck shooting. I love the winter quiet."

"It was not for me to be questioning you," replied Töllong awkwardly. "I am hardly in my right senses yet. Forgive me—it was only that you are so different from the people one expects to meet—no doubt you will be wondering about me—"

"I know one thing. You are a Smålander—"

"My accent betrays me?—yes—"

Töllong was uneasy; he remembered his case and what he had in the pocket of the coat drying before the stove, also his need for haste; then he recalled with pleasure that he *had* crossed the lake; he would, after all, be in time.

"—as long as I am in the city by tonight," he continued.

"That is easy—we are an hour's ride from the suburbs. Your horse struggled ashore—like yourself he is none the worse. The sledge is lost—"

"My case?"

"I fear that has also gone."

Töllong was vexed; but the best place for his papers if they must leave his own possession was the bottom of the lake; again he tried to express his thanks, asked his rescuer's name—

"Gustaf Erikson. I suppose you would have done as much for me." The genial young man seemed amused. "But it was lucky for you I was there. Now you must share my dinner and we will go to the town together. Your clothes will not be dry, but I can lend you others—a servant keeps this place for me, I will send him to you."

As his host left the room Töllong sprang to his furred overcoat, steaming before the stove, and searched nervously in the inner pocket—yes, there was his thick leather wallet almost untouched by the water; on opening it quickly he found, to his great relief, the horn badge of peculiar shape with "Hurry!" cut on it in small letters, his money, and a handsomely engraved ticket for the masquerade at the palace that evening.

His host returned.

"I hope you find your possessions all right?"

Töllong, taken by surprise, laughed awkwardly, vexed at being caught searching in his coat.

"I was anxious, about my money—"

"And that, too, I suppose," added Captain Erikson pointing to the large card embellished with flowers and cupidons that Töllong held. "Forgive me, my friend, but admission to the royal masquerade is not so easily procured—you must be a person of some consequence!"

"I owe it to the kindness of friends," replied Töllong. "Now you understand my reasons for haste—to have gone by the road would have meant missing the ball."

"Which is, however, really not worth risking one's life for," smiled Gustaf Erikson with his strong glance of vivid hazel eyes turned on Töllong. "Though I admit that many of my fellow-officers would have given a great deal—which they don't possess—for a chance to go to such an exclusive affair—at which the King himself will be present."

"Will he, indeed?" replied Töllong, carefully putting away the wallet. "Then I am luckier than I thought."

Captain Erikson's servant entered and opened one of the large pinewood cupboards that lined the wall opposite the stove; this was full of a sufficient variety of garments to prove the soldier to be wealthy and whimsical; for the place was lonely and desolate indeed, yet the wooden house well equipped for a long residence.

As Töllong dressed himself (the two men were much of a size) his host asked him his name and where he should send his own clothes when dry?

"My name is Olaf Brandt and I am staying at The Silver Antlers—but I will not disoblige you any further—I can send for the things tomorrow," he grinned, thinking that tomorrow he would have little need of trifles.

The two men sat down to a meal that Kristian, the servant, prepared and served; with his badge and ticket safe against his heart Töllong felt at ease and even sanguine as to the success of his mission; it was vexatious, of course, that he had roused the curiosity of this amiable stranger who expressed a frank amazement at the young provincial's wild journey to the capital to attend the royal ball—

Töllong also affected to be frank.

"I am under such an obligation to you that it seems churlish to keep secrets—but the friend who has procured me this ticket has done it at some risk—you understand? I must not mention his name."

"A court official?"

Töllong nodded.

"Well, it wouldn't mean much to me! I don't move in those circles—"

Töllong, feeling pressed, admitted:

"Well—the secret isn't mine—forgive me, my friend, the affair is rather delicate!"

"A lady?"

"Precisely! You perceive that my lips are sealed—"

He smiled, knowing that the other thought he insinuated a hint of a love affair, but there was no love in his errand and the lady concerned was long past tenderness or gallantry. When Töllong smiled he was agreeable to look at, for his teeth were even and white and his too vivid blue eyes half closed in a pleasant manner;

his features were harsh, his cheek-bones high and his hair rough and stiff, of the colour of burnt flax; he was splendidly made and had an attractive air of health.

"You ought to be in the army," commented Captain Erikson, probing, Töllong felt, for information.

"I would, maybe, under a different government—"

"Ah, a revolutionary! A republican, what a number there are about!"

"No, no—but one can't have much respect for the present *régime*—"

"You blame the King, no doubt—"

"Well, you can't call him popular, even in the army—"

"Speak freely before me," smiled Gustaf Erikson. "I agree with you that the King is a sad fellow—as much abused in the provinces as in the capital, no doubt."

But Töllong's frankness was nicely calculated, he refused to be drawn further.

"Oh, I haven't thought much about it," he replied.

"I live too remote from politics, I've other things to think of—I'm still a student at Uppsala for one thing and then I help my father with the estates—"

"Ah, you students are dangerous! It is you who write all these wild pamphlets against God and the King—when you have not as much as seen either—"

"Well, I have never written a line in my life—and under your favour, sir, I ought to be getting on."

"I'll swear," smiled the officer, rising, "you are a red-hot '*sans culotte*' or Jacobin—full of advanced ideas and eager to practise 'em!"

"Well," said Töllong, "surely a man of your age isn't satisfied to dry rot in a garrison supporting all the old traditions and conventions and amusing yourself duck shooting in a place like this!"

"I divert myself one way and another, it isn't a bad life, I assure you!" Gustaf Erikson laughed joyously as he slipped into his heavy fur coat; there was something about him, an active grace, a subtle distinction, that was very charming; his easy, friendly manner and an air of generous nobility in his mien tempted Töllong to confidences that he knew he must by no means give. He delighted in the sense of speed given by the swift sledge drive; the young officer had a pair of fine horses and drove at a brisk pace along the level road; as they sped along he talked with great vivacity, smiling over his shoulder above the grey fur of his collar.

Töllong's accident, his brief unconsciousness, his meeting with this charming stranger, had altered his mood; he put his hand over the hidden badge and grinned with excitement; his blue eyes shone with the heartless fervour of the fanatic and his lips, stiff from the cold, formed the word—"hurry!"

Before he crossed the lake he had not paused to think; he had been blindly intent on his errand, almost like an automaton.

Now his mission assumed a sharp importance, because at once richly fantastic, with all the glamour of high adventure, and intensely real, making commonplace incidents appear trivial and intolerably futile.

His blood raced with a keen exhilaration as he saw the towers of the city rise against the cold sky; he, Eügen Töllong, unknown, obscure, with little hope, to the casual observer, of ever being anything else, was entering the capital of his country for the first time utterly unnoticed—but, tomorrow, ah, tomorrow there would be no one in the whole of Sweden who had not heard his name—

"You seem pleased, my friend," remarked Captain Erikson as they drove through the suburbs. "It is true that it is a fine, frosty day, and that you are going to the royal masquerade tonight!"

"But you seem to think there must be a deeper cause for my satisfaction!" smiled Töllong. "Well, I have told you that there is a secret—"

"Which I will not probe—perhaps tomorrow you would like me to show you some of the sights of the city?"

Töllong echoed—"tomorrow!" then added quickly, "Tomorrow I shall have to return."

"So soon! You are indeed a mysterious person! This evening—the masquerade does not begin till midnight—come with me to a little cabaret first—"

Töllong reflected—"I shall have to pass the time somehow—why not with this harmless fellow, who clearly has not a thought beyond his pleasures?" And he agreed to meet the young officer at The Silver Antlers at nine o'clock.

"I have an appointment first, you understand!"

"Ah, with the fair dame, no doubt!"

Töllong nodded; he felt very friendly towards his rescuer though warm feelings were contrary to his nature; but this man had saved his life at risk of his own and at a most opportune moment—if he, Töllong, had gone to the bottom of the lake, how much more than his own life would have been lost!

They parted at the door of Töllong's inn; as the young officer drove gaily away Töllong half regretted that he had made that appointment with him for later in the evening; had he not been warned to beware of all strangers?—"anyone, the most unlikely person, might be a police or government agent in disguise—"; but Töllong reassured himself—the circumstances of his meeting with Gustaf Erikson had been so peculiar—it would have been the oddest coincidence in the world if he had been rescued by an emissary of the government—besides, Erikson was so obviously what he said he was, a careless young officer.

But—no time for reflection—hurry!

The city seemed very gay to him as he started out on his first errand; the fashionable shops, the well-dressed crowds, the tinkle of sledge bells, the darkening blue sky sparkling with clear frost-bright stars all absurdly stimulated Eügen Töllong, the studious provincial.

As he searched for the address he had so carefully committed to memory he came upon a vast building that could be no other than the palace; Töllong stopped dead to stare while passers-by glanced with vexation at his large bulk and rustic obstruction of the pavement.

The lamps of festival were already being hung in the windows of the palace, the last light of day showed the evening wind lifting the folds of the royal standard on the topmost tower... Töllong felt himself part of great events. He found his destination to be an old timber house in a quiet square; there were gooseberry bushes in the patch of garden, he noticed the tiny first leaves among the long thorns.

The door opened at once to his five carefully spaced knocks; he showed his horn badge and was admitted by a fellow who might have been any servant in any service.

Töllong followed him up the narrow stairs into a plain room shuttered against the twilight. Three men, all strangers to Töllong, sat round a deal table lit by a cheap lamp; one was corpulent and slovenly in his person, one a dandy, gaunt and high shouldered, the third elderly, withered and bowed; their faces Töllong could not see, for they wore masks.

He stood before them, his badge in his hand; knowing that he was being keenly scrutinised; with an effort at ease he said:

"You are the members of the Committee to whom I was to report?"

"We are," replied the stout man. "And you are Eügen Töllong whom we were to expect?"

"Yes—is there any need for mystery, gentlemen? Surely I have proved that I am to be trusted?"

"No doubt," answered the other dryly, "or you would not be here. But why wish to burden yourself with the knowledge of our identities? What you do not know you cannot reveal."

Without waiting for any possible comment he continued:

"We have examined your *dossier*, you seem in all suitable. You have no regrets, fears or scruples?"

"None," Töllong declared vehemently. "When I was told that the lot had fallen to me, I prepared to put myself absolutely at your disposal—"

"You know what you risk?"

"Of course." Töllong's wrought-up fanaticism was scornful of this prosy talk; the masks glanced at each other, approving his resolute carriage; the oldest handed him a packet.

"Very well, no need for further talk when we all understand each other perfectly. Here are your instructions, your costume and domino will be delivered at your inn."

To this the stout man added:

"Madame wishes to see you first—"

Töllong bowed; the third man, who had not yet spoken, offered him a glass of brandy which he drank—"to the health of our enterprise". The cold had been so intense on his journey that he had not touched alcohol since he left home, the spirit therefore sent his blood racing and made his mood even more buoyant; he felt a hero and a martyr; his face, frostbitten on the nose arch and cheek-bones, set in an expression of cold ferocity, the relentless grimace of the fanatic.

The three conspirators, looking at him, were satisfied with the skilful jugglery that had made the name of Eügen Töllong appear on the ticket drawn from so many others, the man was made for his purpose—no need to fear that he would not carry it through.

They questioned him about his journey—he had had a long way to travel since he had received the message that his had been the name drawn.

Töllong said nothing about that adventure at the lake; it now seemed a rather ridiculous kind of miracle; he would not waste time recounting such futilities—besides, he did not wish to admit that his papers were at the bottom of the ice-bound waters.

"At twelve o'clock someone will call for you," remarked the most elegant of the masks; he rose, as if dismissing Töllong, but added:

"One formality—you will take the customary oath that nothing whatever will turn you from your purpose—"

"Easily—what could turn me?"

"Nothing, as we hope. Remember, *nothing*, not the most unforeseen, most fantastic circumstance—swear." Raising his right hand to heaven, Töllong swore.

"You are the saviour of your country!" exclaimed the stout man, embracing him.

Töllong was outside in the cold night, in the obscure little garden; a sharp subtle fragrance came from the gooseberry bushes, the moon, nearly at the full, was rising above the dark lines of the roofs.

He hastened back to his inn; his domino had arrived; a lavender-blue Venetian cloak with a white mask and black hat; with it was a suit of violet velvet.

Töllong laid all ready in his room, locked the door and went down to dinner in the public ordinary.

The place was full and he heard a good deal of revolutionary talk; how quickly these new ideas spread, how free they were in the capital! In the provinces one had to be circumspect, but here every topic was openly criticised, every public personage abused, the example of France, of America, freely admired; "*A bas les tyrants!*"; everyone seemed full of intoxicating hope, of relentless vigour; what a marvellous new world was to rise from the ruins of the old!

Töllong with difficulty restrained himself from joining in this patriotic hubbub, especially when the King was abused, ah, he, too, knew something of that evil monarch.

Slightly lowering their voices the two men at the nearest table gloated over the vices, the extravagances, the insolences of the King; all the faults of a corrupt government were laid at his door; so headstrong, too, and infatuate.

"Can't he see when he is going too far?"

"We want another Brutus—"

"The old Queen-mother now, she knows what she is about—she has up-to-date ideas."

Töllong drank another glass of brandy, but no more; he must, of all things, be sober tonight; but sober was what he could not be, for the strange events through which he was passing intoxicated him without the help of spirits.

Boisterously he hailed Captain Erikson, who drove up his spanking greys exact to the minute.

"You city folk are pretty cool! The people here talk boldly of the most delicate subjects—even railing against the King—"

"Oh, that's nothing! One hears that kind of conversation at any mess table—it is rather the fashion. Rousseau, Voltaire, Danton! Come along, I will take you to a cabaret where you will hear some fine spouting!"

"Do you, an officer of the garrison, dare to frequent such haunts?" asked Töllong, springing in beside the other as the sledge took the street again, sending the powdered snow flying.

"Oh, the city is very badly policed, one does what one likes! It is easy to see that everything goes to pieces!"

"It seems to me," said Töllong, settling under the warm fur rugs, "that the King must be not only a scoundrel, but an imbecile!"

"Very likely—they say he is certain to be assassinated one of these days."

Töllong startled:

"He takes no precautions?"

"Eh, how do I know!" replied the young officer, who seemed indeed a wild, reckless fellow. "But why do you call him a scoundrel? Has he ruined your sister, seduced your wife, or cast your old father into prison?"

"Bah, he has never heard of my existence—but everyone knows he is a scoundrel—"

"I have heard him sometimes called a reformer—"

"Nonsense, he is a contemptible tyrant." Töllong spoke casually. "Why should we concern ourselves with him! Perhaps the old Queen is more to your mind—she is always quarrelling with him—"

"I know nothing about her," lied Töllong.

The sledge drew up at an obscure cabaret; the windows sent long rays of yellow light on to the piled snow without; a porter sprang out to seize the reins, Töllong followed his friend into noise, warmth, a close atmosphere of food and wine odours, then into a crowded inner room where the company greeted Gustaf Erikson with lusty pleasure.

"I must be cautious," Töllong told himself, "or these half-drunken fools will delay me."

Seizing him by the arm Erikson shouted:

"Here is Olaf Brandt whom I fished out of the lake this morning—he was frozen as stiff as a radish! A fine introduction to Stockholm! But—what do you think, this lucky devil has a ticket for the masquerade tonight!"

"I have a friend at court," Töllong hastened to explain. "No names, gentlemen, you understand!"

He sat down in the chair pulled out for him; he had a pleasant feeling of dominating them all, that there was something in his air, his glance that betrayed his full and magnificent life, his powerful purpose which was soon to sweep up to a dramatic climax that would startle the whole of Europe, yes, soon the whole world would hear of Eügen Töllong!

"Come!" cried Erikson. "What is the subject for debate tonight! Was it not to be that man should live to his full capacity—regardless of commendation and convention?"

By this Töllong learned that he had been introduced into some manner of club and one which, despite the presence of several officers, was of a revolutionary tendency; many of those crowded round the table began to talk together; how full of eagerness and vivacity they were, how they clamoured for youth, youth! Away with the old men, away with the middle-aged men, away with all mouldering tradition, sentiment, and rules!

There were several pretty women present; and they were loudest of all in their enthusiastic outcry; one, of a flamboyant beauty, sat next Töllong, crowded up to him in the press; her bosom was bare, a fur hat was tied under her chin, she continually offered to touch glasses with Töllong, inviting him to drink, but he remembered the badge on his breast—"hurry!"

Through the tobacco smoke showed a clock painted with pale, sickly sentimental wreaths of blue and pink flowers; Töllong watched the minutes tick away on the bland face of this timepiece; he must be wary, sober, quick.

He closed his eyes, overwhelmed by a spasm of giddiness; he seemed to be floundering in the black, icy water again, being sucked under the dark blue ice floes; he heard Erikson vehemently, with reckless gaiety, talking this wild modern talk—he, Eügen Töllong, ought to love that man who had saved him for such a glorious destiny—

"Man's utmost capabilities!" cried Erikson; "who knows if he is not a potential hero or murderer!"

"Perhaps it is the same thing," said Töllong's neighbour, nudging him.

He opened his eyes; the heated faces crowded round the table looked grotesque—some seemed even to assume animal shapes, foxes, wolves, ferrets—only the amiable countenance of Gustaf Erikson remained charming, ingenuous amid the hurly-burly.

Töllong struggled to his feet amid burst of laughter; there were shouts of "Speech! Speech!"

Was it possible, he wondered, that he was becoming light-headed, or even a little drunk, or that the submersion in the lake had left a fever in his blood?

"I must get away," he declared—"this is all very amusing, but while you are all talking I have work to do—"

The fair woman at his side tried to detain him.

"What work, tell us; we are all friends here!"

"I thought you were going to the masquerade!" cried another.

They all laughed again; insanely, Töllong thought; the circle of faces began to dip and reel before him, the insipid dial of the clock seemed to simper through that idiotic wreath of pallid flowers.

"Hurry!" said Töllong under his breath, and broke through the room; laughter followed him; he hurried across the outer parlour; a drunkard, still clasping a pewter pot, was being thrown out; Töllong broke into the open air; ah, that was better!

The fresh, clear cold after the stale heat of the stove, the sting of the frosty wind on one's face, the icy sparkle of the stars overhead—now the high heroic purpose showed definite again.

The snow was beautiful in the light from the tavern window, the pure white drifts flushed with amber gold; Töllong hurried; the city was splendid about him, rich, darkling; he saw nothing squalid nor vile.

Back again in his room at The Silver Antlers he changed into the carnival suit and cloak; at midnight precisely a stranger, a sober sad-looking man, called for him; another sledge was at the door, two impatient horses—ah, that was it, movement, perpetual movement!—hurry, hurry, towards the great climax!

"You have your ticket?" asked the muffled man beside him as they drove to the palace.

"Yes."

"You will be admitted to the ball by a side entrance—but the police are very watchful just now—every mask may be asked to show his ticket—"

"I am in every way prepared—"

"No hesitancies, no regrets of any kind, no tremors, Eügen Töllong?"

"None," he replied, thinking how famous that name would be tomorrow.

The palace suddenly towered over them, blocking out the stars; a figure sprang out from the shadows to seize the reins, the two jumped out, skirted the wall, entered by a small door, crossed the garden and were in the grandiose building.

A narrow dark staircase led to a plainly furnished room overheated by a white porcelain stove; a parrot slept in an ebony ring, a length of linen embroidered in gold sequins trailed over a hooded chair.

Töllong struggled against a sense of unreality; too many varied scenes had he been hurried through in the last few hours; he could scarcely control his exalted mood. His companion, looking at him sharply, demanded: "Are you ill? Do your spirits, after all, fail?"

"No, no."

"Follow me, then—and be circumspect—"

Another room hung with grey serge in sign of mourning, a huge bed with black posts and tufts of sable plumes above the crape canopy on which the dust lay heavily; a stove of dark glaze with the grate pulled open showing the fire as red as hell—an old woman in a great chair wearing the monstrous head-dress of twenty years before.

Töllong went on one knee and the lady held out a withered hand covered with ugly jewellery.

"So—you are he!" she exclaimed eagerly, "and the moment has come at last!"

"I am, Madame, ready."

Töllong gazed with veneration at the repulsive old hag; she had reigned beside Sweden's greatest King during the golden age of splendid victory, of freedom and progress; for years she had been a prisoner in the hands of the brood descended from her husband's disastrous first marriage with the false intriguing Latin; her own children had been exiled or slain.

But even in her great age she preserved the spirit and energy of her youth and was the linch-pin of numerous conspiracies; all had been unsuccessful and followed by bloody reprisals, all save this last skilful plot, long in maturing.

The ancient Queen, who had been for so long an historic figure, a relic of the gorgeous past, an inspiration for an even more gorgeous future, was a hideous enough figure in her painted decrepitude, her lean head nodding with palsy, her lips drawn up like a purse with a string, her whistling voice.

But Töllong bowed before her courage, her race, her patriotism.

"Odd," she grinned, "that this great work should come into the hands of a raw young provincial like you—hold up your head and let me look at you!"

"The lot fell to me, Madame."

HURRY! HURRY!

Töllong raised his gaunt face, so hard in outline for all his youth; the harsh blue eyes over-vivid with the blaze of fanaticism.

"You'll do," chuckled the Queen. "Though they say he has the devil's luck, it should desert him this time!"

"I do not see how I can possibly fail."

The old woman nodded with approval; she had great dignity; it was astonishing to reflect how many tragedies she had seen, how many delusions and disappointments she had survived.

"You will be the liberator of your country," she said, "but very likely you will never hear anyone call you that—"

Töllong on one knee before her, in his fantastic garb, felt love of life well into his heart; he suddenly recalled, with intense regret, the fleshly young woman who had sat next him in the cabaret; again he seemed to be beneath the lake, in blackness under the ice; the old voice came from a distance.

"Some women would not have avowed themselves to you—but my House has never lacked courage. I wished to thank you, to assure you that you will rid the country of a tyrant, a vicious, cruel, blasphemous wretch."

Töllong opened his eyes; this sounded like the talk in the cabaret; the old creature was sunk into her hooded chair; there was something disgusting about her intense vitality; why should she any longer care about the disposition of kingdoms?

Töllong wished that he had not seen her; she gave him her blessing; God, she was sure, would give His benison to the deed that would put her son on the throne.

A widow for forty years, she had lived shut away in deepest mourning—the day that her husband's grandson was no more her dismal rooms would be hung with ruddy brocade.

She babbled on; Töllong's companion whispered the password—"Hurry!" in his ear; he rose, thinking that she had forgotten his presence, but, as he was departing, she said clearly:

"If you *can* escape—remember your way here, I would hide you—perhaps, after all, you may live to be a hero!"

Töllong was conducted down long, dim corridors; on one side were large circular windows wreathed with massive alabaster fruit; Töllong peered through one of these into the ballroom below.

The masquerade, which was to continue until seven in the morning, had begun.

A low delicate fountain cast glittering drops into a pool lit by faint coloured lamps; on the strong jets little scarlet balls danced; round this, in the centre of the great ballroom moved the masks in elaborate disguises.

Invisible musicians provided delicious music, at once rich and fine; buffets placed against the walls of blue-veined alabaster were heaped with sweetmeats and *corbeilles* of hot-house peaches, nectarines, muscat grapes and gnarled melons, wreathed by garlands of jasmine and orange blossoms.

The crowd perpetually moved to and fro, and perpetually laughed.

Töllong peered from behind the carvings of the circular window at which no one thought to glance up.

His companion, gazing over his shoulder, whispered: "That is he, in the purple red domino with the white lining—"

"Can you be absolutely sure?"

"I am his valet," replied the sad-faced man. "I put it on him myself."

Töllong startled.

"Is he as much hated as that?"

He thought it an ugly thing that a man's own body-servant should betray him.

"And to make everything quite certain," continued the servant in an even lower whisper, "I put a little ruby brooch, that he is quite unaware of himself, in the back of the collar of his cloak."

"I shall make no mistake," grinned Töllong.

"Now I must go, lest I am found missing from my post."

He crept away, down the corridor, and Eügen Töllong's gaze followed through the shifting, brilliant crowd the man whom he had hastened across the country to assassinate.

Everything had gone smoothly; so much intelligence, care and skilful organisation had gone to make it possible for him to be here, in the royal palace with a long, sharp, fine knife under his cloak ready to rid Sweden of the tyrant who flaunted so securely below.

So many plots had been discovered, but this would not be; so many attempts on the King's life had been foiled, but this would not be—

The man sauntering among his guests below was as surely doomed as if steel was already next his ribs.

Töllong leant his head against the rich window frame; queer waves of giddiness swept over him, he was now hot, now cold; he shivered though the palace was luxuriously warm.

He refused to admit that he was excited; it must be a touch of fever following his accident; but he could not deny that he began, for the first time, to realise that he intended to murder a fellow creature. Yes, he had considered himself utterly without heart or conscience in this affair, but now—bah! he must be ill!

Grimly controlling himself, he deliberately noted the way he had come from the old Queen's apartments—she had said she would hide him—that would be his one chance of escape—but he must not think of himself.

It was easy to reach the ballroom; as he descended the stairs where several revellers had strayed, he saw, through a window of clear glass, fireworks rising and falling across the park; the beauty, the gaiety of these artificial suns and stars in green, violet, gold and ruby added to his excitement, which was increased by the gorgeous spectacle in which he found himself when he entered the ballroom—never had he seen anything so splendid.

Here, opulent, insolent and still supreme was the world which men like himself had sworn to destroy—here was what all the people in The Silver Antlers, in the cabaret, had raved against—how imposing it was, how august, how, in some subtle way, different from that gross luxury, that wasteful extravagance that Töllong had so often heard so ferociously denounced; now it seemed impossible that there could be anything sinful in what was so rich, so exquisite—

He was touched on the arm; the password "Hurry!" was whispered in his ear under cover of the sweet incessant music; he followed the scarlet domino who had spoken into an alcove where gilded alabaster statues of the Three Graces poured scented water into a silver basin.

The mask, whose voice Töllong recognised as the stout member of the Committee, said:

"You have seen him?"

"Yes, yes," whispered Töllong. "I have never lost sight of him—but there is no chance of a mistake? He has not changed dominoes with anyone? I have heard of such things—"

"Be at ease—to make all certain—I will call him aside and tell him something so startling that he will raise his vizard—"

"But I do not know him!"

"I do," the corpulent man chuckled; evidently he was a great personage about the court—"if it is he I will say the one word—'hurry!'—and you will strike—"

"Very well." Töllong was shuddering to his heart. "But what can you tell him to so move him!"

The other laughed grossly.

"I shall tell him I have discovered a plot to assassinate him! That's a good joke, eh? You have all ready? A firm blow, remember, though his cloak is only light silk—"

Töllong felt sunk in waves of perfume, of music that blended into the icy waters of the lake; he saw a woman unmask in the recess behind the alabaster statues; she laughed into the hidden visage of her companion; there were big diamonds round her throat.

"That is the Princess Ulrica, the King's sister—she does as much evil as he; afterwards—she must be disposed of."

"Extraordinary," muttered Töllong. "I thought I saw her in a cabaret tonight among a party of revolutionaries—"

"You must keep your wits about you better—"

The scarlet domino moved away; Eügen Töllong thought that the Princess was looking at him; he put up a prayer both for himself and the man he was about to kill, and again he had the sensation of water closing over him; icy currents that were yet perfumed, cracking floes that gave out the music of violins, a cruel ice maiden lurking in the depths who had the features of the woman in the cabaret, of the Princess Ulrica... of his evil spirit.

The scarlet and the purple-red domino entered the alcove together; Töllong fixed his gaze on the brooch of rubies on the deep silk collar—how many inches below that must he strike?

He slipped behind the simpering statues; the woman had moved away; he was distracted by the sight of her gauzy fan she had left behind; he heard the conspirator say:

"Sire—this is deeply important—a plot against your life—I must be assured that it is His Majesty to whom I speak—"

"Surely you cannot mistake me, my dear councillor, even in a mask!" But as he uttered these words the speaker raised his vizard and his companion at once ejaculated: "Hurry!"

Töllong sprang forward, his knife in his hand; it did not seem possible then that any miracle could have saved the King.

But Töllong's raised arm fell to his side, the knife dropped at his feet, with a horrid exclamation he turned and stumbled away.

In the face the King turned on him he had recognised the candid, amiable countenance of Gustaf Erikson.

He was conscious of a hubbub, a shrieking behind him; he groaned in the hysterical anguish of the realisation of his own deception as he fled through the silken crowd, pushing aside garlands from porticoes.

It was he, not the tyrant, who was doomed to die tonight—ah, he understood how that wicked man had fooled him—stolen his papers, looked through his pockets—led him on, wickedly disguised, with his evil sister, knowing that at the supreme moment he, Eügen Töllong, would be unable to strike the man who had saved his life.

He dare not think of the hundreds he had betrayed by his cowardice, of the heroic old Queen impatient to proclaim him "hero," of all those waiting for a signal that now would never be given—"Hurry!" not to another's end but to his own; he and not the King had been doomed when the lot was drawn.

He flung aside his mask, his domino—all disguise was useless—and fled down the frozen path, embracing the imaginary waters that closed over his head; the hubbub was behind him; before him the fireworks soared and scattered; he saw them beneath his feet, he was near water then; without pause he flung himself headlong; his plunge broke the reflected glories of the sham stars; a panting crowd with lanterns gathered round the stone edge of the artificial lake, jostling each other in the bewildering light and shade.

Councillor ——, panting behind the King, who seemed to regard the whole affair as a jest, thought, very bitterly:

"How is it that they all fail when it comes to the scratch! He seemed such a likely fellow—and to lose his head so desperately! It is true that I am not able to do it myself—"

Eügen Töllong was dragged out of the pretty little pond and laid at the feet of the King; his teeth were showing, his harsh hair stuck out in spikes; he looked like a drowned wolf; the Princess Ulrica shrieked, but gazed greedily.

"Conscience makes cowards of us all," quoted a pedant solemnly; the King said:

"Bah! the fellow was mad!"

Both were right; the King never knew that he owed his life to a slight likeness he bore to one Gustaf Erikson who at that moment was enjoying himself in a cabaret where revolutionary doctrines were discussed.

The festival crowd dispersed from about the corpse which was fast becoming frozen; all shuddered back to the warmth, the music, the perfumes; even his fellow-conspirators were glad to forsake Eügen Töllong.

"How quickly he died!" one whispered with horror. But Töllong had been dying since he had received the command to murder.

SHEEP'S-HEAD
AND BABYLON

The Reverend Zachary Barlas opened the door of the manse and entered with a flagging step.

It was a melancholy day in deep winter, and the wind howled incessantly through the hills, across the moor and beat into the little garden of the manse, (in summer rich with honeysuckle and roses) and on to the unsheltered square walls of the building itself, and up the struggling village street through which the minister had just come with his slow and uneasy walk. It was no earthly trouble that made the Rev. Zachary look haggard and pallid, but prolonged wrestling with spiritual hosts and exhausting struggles with diabolic terrors.

It was indeed only what he had to expect, for he had long been devoting his austere leisure to the writing of a book entitled "The Snares of Satan Exposed," which must certainly be highly displeasing to the Father of Evil, since it so learnedly, succinctly and clearly exposed his traps and wiles, and was a kind of chart or guide to the unwary to avoid the pitfalls set by the legions of the Infernal One.

Long and late had the Rev. Zachary laboured at this work, putting into it a burning zeal, an exalted piety and the fervent outpourings of a devoted heart, and now that his work was nearing completion he felt an exhaustion of the spirit, a feebleness of the body not surprising, for, besides the book into which he had put such passionate ardour, he had toiled ceaselessly in his tiny parish, preaching, exhorting, tending the sick, the penitent and the sinner, encouraging the worthy, comforting the distressed; for a holy and fearless man was he, albeit stern and unrelenting.

As he crossed the threshold of the manse the wind sent a dismal sigh through a leafless ash tree that overhung the house, and the minister shivered; the thought of his book lying upstairs, finished save for the last few pages, gave him, however, a sense of chill triumph; he had put through his appointed task, and the Devil had not been able to prevent him. Indeed, he believed that the invisible powers that had been harrying him had given up a vain pursuit, for during several days he had been conscious of a certain calm in the atmosphere in which he moved, an atmosphere hitherto filled with a wild commotion as of spirits battling for his soul.

As he passed down the narrow passage he peeped in at the kitchen, with the yellow sanded floor and the bright pots and pans and the pleasant fire.

On the freshly scrubbed table was the food prepared for his supper: a bundle of herbs, a winter cabbage and a sheep's head.

The minister stood still and gazed at the sheep's head.

It was a drab white colour with great curling horns, a long beard that hung over the edge of the table and slant eyes that appeared still to glow with life.

"Maisie!" cried the minister, and his thin voice failed in his withered throat.

The maid, a big bustling woman with horseshoe shaped mutch on her head, appeared instantly from an inner room, her red hands dripping with fresh cold water.

"Maisie," said the minister, "I no like the look of yon sheep's head. It's ower long in the beard, and ower powerfu' in the horns, and unco' cunning in the eyes for the hoose of an honest mon."

"Losh!" cried the old woman, and "Gude save us!" she cried. "What daftlike thing is this? 'Twas the bit wench brought it in, and she'll e'en tak it back."

"It's gey and queerish," added the minister slowly.

"It's a willie goat," said Maisie, sniffing the head; "an unearthly rank smell it has, and it's no the meat for a Christian hoose."

"Boil the pot with a bit of beef," replied the minister, "the thing is no canny."

Slowly he went upstairs, thinking dourly of Tam Todd the butcher who had sent such an unsightly object to the manse, and shuddering as the cleaving wind swept down from the hills and across the bleak moor, curdling the loch and the rivulet into spate and whistling through the crevices in the manse walls. On his neat desk were his neat papers, and he seized on them with lean hands.

"That was an unearthly sign," he muttered; "a Jeroboam among sheep! Sheep, did I say? Maybe sae. Maybe sae. But strang is the hand of God! He no let ony sic a mischanter come ower me noo!" Yet he looked round fearfully, prying into every corner of the room and fingering his sharp chin.

It was very cold in this upper room; the icicles hung on the pane, the madly-fleeing east wind was carrying the first snowflakes past the window.

"There's a fire bleezing awa in the parlour," came Maisie's voice up the narrow stairs, "an' all tosh and comfortable. Wull ye no come down and tak the bit supper?"

"Have ye sent back the deil's heid to the auld carlin that sent it?" demanded the minister.

"It's gone awa," came the screaming reply, "and blessings on it, no the deil, but a willie goat; and dinna fash yersel, I'll get as fine a heid of sheep as ever fed on Cheviot."

"A foolish, doited body," muttered the minister, "do ye no speir the deil's trick through the hands of that puir body Tam Todd? And dinna ye ken the likeness of the Father of Evil when it lies before ye?"

He turned his back again to his desk; neither meal nor fire nor toddy-glass had any attraction for him, save as temptations to be gloriously resisted.

"I maun finish," he said, lovingly taking up his pen, "for the deil's on my tracks. And what needeth man with food when his innards are burnt up with a fervent heat which is the love of the Lord?"

Crouching his limbs together in his rusty black single-breasted coat, his Cameron breeches, darned stockings and square-toed shoes, propping his meagre face on his hollowed and claw-like hand, Zachary Barlas gazed at the flying storm that leapt past the window and concentrated on his final chapters.

He was writing a vision of Babylon, the City of Sin, the capital of the country called Destruction, circled about by the moat filled with the waters of despair and warmed by the fires of hell.

"Babylon," he wrote, "is not a place, but a state; to be in sin is to be in Babylon; to be in temptation is to be lingering at the gates."

Soaring above the homely vernacular in which he daily expressed himself, the Rev. Zachary launched into the florid and robust diction drawn from the writings of the Covenanters, flushed and glorified by the splendours of the Bible—the Holy Book that lay open at his elbow, and at which he often glanced with a pale but sparkling eye.

As he wrote he forgot the cold, forgot the storm sweeping down from Craigie Sauchie, forgot the disdained comforts of food and warmth below.

"This great city, this glorious city, this rich city, this mighty powerful city, this queen of the earth, with Antichrist, her king and husband, is to be judged by the spirit of life, which ariseth out of the dust of Sion."

Soft the snow thudded on the window, cramped and frozen were the blue fingers of the minister, but unfalteringly flowed the eager words on to the paper.

"Sing, sing, O inhabitant of Sion! Dost thou not perceive the crown of pride going down apace? The decree sealed against her; she cannot escape; yea, she is fallen, she is fallen, she is already taken in the snow; the eye of my life seeth it and rejoiceth over her in the living power."

The minister sank back in his mean chair, his eyes rolled in his head, and he broke into emphatic speech:

"'Fear God and give glory to Him, for the hour of His judgment is come!'" he cried, adding: "an' ye canna escape! ye canna escape!"

The little room was darkening in the winter twilight; fleeting wind and gathering snow made one commotion outside; the white drift was piling high on the window-sill and blotting the murky pane.

"A beam o' light, O Lord!" prayed the Rev. Zachary, "for the place darkens!"

He rose, but his limbs were stiff and his pace was stumbling; indeed the room seemed to be full of a deep gloom which rendered the objects in it nearly indistinguishable. Whether this was due to the thickening of the storm without or the failing of his own senses the minister did not know. He pulled open the door.

Instead of the mean, shabby staircase of the manse he saw before him a passage of shimmering gold, washed by a pale and unearthly light.

"Babylon!" whispered the Rev. Zachary, and, irritated by this device of the Evil One, he turned to reach the safe harbourage of his chill workroom; but the door had disappeared.

The long gold street was in front and behind him; to his left was a wall of jasper or some translucent material, crowned at intervals with turrets of silver hung with hundreds of little silver bells that clashed gently in an eternal breeze. On the other side tall straight buildings of a milky alabaster rose till they disappeared in the rosy clouds.

There were deep-set windows latticed with ivory and high doors curtained with satin in these houses, and long festoons of roses falling from golden balconies; the air was drowsy with the scents of jasmine, of honeysuckle, of musk, and alive with the sounds of sackbut, dulcimer and zither. The minister felt like a drab insect drawling over a luscious fruit.

Yet he was able to show his contempt for the Devil by walking straight on with no glance to right or left.

"I'll walk clean through yon gaudy show," he said, "and back to my wee bit room."

A door opened with a soft sliding sound and a woman peeped out; a flimsy lawn barely veiled the palpitations of her delicate bosom, long strands of golden hair escaped from a fillet of white roses, and over her polished bare shoulders hung a cloak of royal purple.

"It is far from Drumknockie Manse to Babylon," she said. "Will you not come in and rest?"

So sweet and beguiling was her accent, so delicious the perfume that wafted from the open door, so entrancing the glimpse of the soft couch within and the display of exquisite viands on a table of pure jade, that the Rev. Zachary actually paused.

"I must not eat or rest in Babylon," he muttered. But he fingered his chin and sighed, and many things became dim in his mind.

"Many a holy man has rested here before you," smiled the lady, "and passed on his way much refreshed."

The Rev. Zachary gazed at her dewy lips, her blooming cheeks, her sapphire eyes, and he forgot he was in Babylon.

His hand went out, wavered and strayed towards the lovely lady's heavy locks.

"I might—rest—a while," he stammered, and stepped on to the threshold. Then he glanced down, dazzled, maybe, by the brightness of the lady's charms; and what did he behold?

A neat little goat's foot—white, it is true, as to hair, and shell-pink as to horn, but indubitably a goat's foot—peeping out under the purple cloak.

And what did he see on the table among the costly meats and delicate drinks?

The sheep's head, with the beard and the horns, leering at him with half-closed eyes.

The Rev. Zachary groaned.

"Sathanas, avaunt!" he cried desperately.

The golden city melted about him; he seemed to pitch into an abyss, and found himself on his hands and knees, sprawling down his own stairs.

"Guid save us!" cried Maisie, running out, "and what cantrips are these? Coming down heid formaist! Losh, but it's a ghaistly sicht!"

The minister sat at the bottom of the stairs and rubbed his elbows.

"Maisie," he mumbled, "I've been to Babylon—it was a maist ungodly sicht! Streets o' gowd, an' a woman—"

"I'll no hear about the woman," retorted Maisie firmly. "If ye've been to Babylon, it's no the women o' that city will be the decent talk for a Christian buddy."

The minister rose stiffly from his sitting posture and limped towards the parlour.

"Ye're ower lang at the writing," said the housekeeper, anxiously following him into the light and warmth; "tak a drap and a bite noo."

She pointed to the supper displayed temptingly on the hearth.

But the Rev. Zachary remembered the invitation extended to him recently by a fairer favoured damsel.

"It's no the willie goat?" he asked, glancing at the covered dish.

"The willie goat?" replied Maisie scornfully. "Has na the willie goat gone back to auld Tam Todd?"

"I'm glad," replied the minister. He sank down in the old armchair by the cheerful fire and ate his supper with a quiet relish.

He felt great cause for rejoicing. Had he not passed down the very streets of Babylon and returned unscathed? Had he not withstood temptations as successfully as St. Anthony himself (who was but a Papist, after all!) and returned safe and sound to eat his own food by his own fireside? "Surely," he thought, "the Devil has done with me now, and left me in peace." Flushed with a sense of exultation he climbed again to his workroom, and, albeit a little stiff from his fall, he seized his pen with fervour and in a kind of delirium of zeal finished the last few pages of his book.

"Auld Mahoun nearly had me that time—I was half-way hame to his cauldron, nae doot," he muttered triumphantly as he tied up the thick pile of manuscript; "and mony hae travelled that road afore me, as the Scarlet Woman herself testified with her soft words and wanton looks."

The wind whirled round the house and cast thuds of snow at the windows and whistled icy breaths through the crevices as the Rev. Zachary went downstairs to his warm and sheltered, if grim and dour, parlour.

Casting his haggard eyes upwards in self-congratulatory praise, he took down from the shelf that formed his meagre library a big Bible bound in black oak and clasped with silver; he turned over the pages with gaunt fingers and muttered over the familiar passages with which he had often rebuked sin and hurled at the abomination of witchcraft and devilry.

With these forces he had held many a dubious and fierce conflict; on the hills above Drumknockie were the ruins of a Runic temple, well known to be still the abode of unclean spirits, and on the coast not far distant was a wrecked ship, stuck in the quicksands, that had sailed from the haunted coast of Norway, and was still the abode of ghastly spectres; of these things the Rev. Zachary was thinking as he thumbed his Bible and listened to the storm. Yet he felt as secure in his triumph as any of the lonely Covenanters lying in the solitary graves among the hills had felt in their faith.

Had he not actually visited Babylon and rejected it, together with the lure of the Scarlet Woman?

He was totally absorbed in these pleasing reflections when old Maisie opened the door and peeped in, with a look of awed respect for his devotions.

"There's a bit lassie at the door, begging to see you, and saying she's in sair trouble, and has great need of a douce and godly man."

The heart of the pastor swelled with pride; secure as a watcher on the tower of Judah, he ordered the wench to be brought in. It was always a joy to him to receive penitents and wrestle with crime, sin and folly, and many a redoubtable battle of this kind had been fought out in the dreary little parlour.

"But it's an awfu' night for a lassie to be abroad," he added as another shrieking gust shook the house.

"The lassie," replied Maisie, lowering her voice, "has the snood weel ower her face; but I shouldn't wonder if it were Geordie Murray's daughter, and she'll nae hae far to gang."

The pastor was surprised, for the girl in question lived next door, in one of the better cottages of the village, and was the daughter of a decent shepherd, and but a child in years.

"Aweel, bring her in," he said, and, with the Bible still open on his knee, he waited.

Maisie showed into the parlour a young girl whose maiden snood was drawn well over her face, and whose plaid was huddled closely round her shoulders; her feet were bare, her skirt short, and she carried a bundle wrapped in a white cloth which she at once placed on the table.

The Rev. Zachary saw that his visitor indeed was Jessie Murray, the light-hearted child he had so often seen pulling gowans on the hills and singing at her spinning wheel.

"Oh, I'm in sair trouble," she said, clasping her hands, "sair trouble! What am I brocht to?"

The pastor observed that Jessie, though she had only run a few yards through the storm, was pale and shivering with cold, and drifts of snow already lay in her snood and plaid.

"What for will ye no warm yerself, Jessie Murray?" said the pastor, "and shake the snow frae ye wee plaid? I'm a wearifu' mon tonight, but I'm aye ready for a gude deed."

With a deep sigh the girl took off her plaid, loosened her wet snood, sending a shower of auburn curls on to her shoulders, and knelt before the glowing fire.

"Sic a nicht to gang about in!" she said in a low voice, "the snaw drifting, the stars a' put out and a spate in the river, and maybe the Faither o' Lies riding the clouds!"

The tempest had indeed reached a terrific pitch; the shriek of the wind had a human quality, like the screams of tormented voices, and the manse literally quivered on its foundations.

"Preserve us a'!" exclaimed the pastor, gripping the Bible tighter.

"An' dinna ye think it's ower powerfu' for a storm?" whispered Jessie.

"And what wud it be?" demanded the Rev. Zachary. "An'," he added, with a rising voice, "gin it waur the Devil at his tantrums, I'm the maister! Sae dinna be frightened."

Thus encouraged, Jessie clasped her hands on her bosom and, crouching nearer to the minister's chair, stammered out her story.

"I'm sair afraid—my father awa'—and I biding in the hoose, when who should come but a bit laddie to the door, through the storm and a', and slippit into my hand—"

She broke off and glanced fearfully at the covered bundle she had placed on the table.

"'It's the wee meat frae Tam Todd,' says he, and rins awa'—and what is it?"

As she spoke she snatched away the cloth and displayed to the amazed gaze of the minister the sheep's head he had seen on his own kitchen table.

"Sic doings!" he exclaimed. "But be no afeard, lassie—'tis but a willie goat which that miserable creature, Tam Todd, wad pass off as gude Christian meat—gang hame and tak it wi' ye, and think nae mair o't."

"But I'm afeard to take it up!" cried Jessie, "and afeard to gang hame in sic a storm!"

The Rev. Zachary gazed at the head on the table; it was a fearsome sight with the shining curling horns, the drab mottled fur, the long beard and the glinting eyes, and wrath grew in the minister's breast at the impudence of the butcher who persisted in delivering this unsavoury object at the houses of honest folk.

While he was considering the stern terms of rebuke he would administer on the morrow he felt his knees softly clasped and the lassie clinging to him.

"I'm cauld," she murmured, "cauld, cauld, and sair afeard."

The Rev. Zachary looked down at her; he had never remembered that the child was so lovely, so dewy bright, so glowing and soft. As he gazed into the upturned face, the glittering curls falling beside the rounded throat and over the white shoulders, and the delicate bosom swelling beneath the cotton kerchief, the Bible slipped from his knees and crashed unheeded to the floor.

"You're ower lovely for Jessie Murray," he murmured. "But gang awa'—put yon heid in your apron and gang hame."

But the girl did not move; nay, she clung tighter to the minister's knees, and moaned and sobbed while the wind shook and shrilled.

The Rev. Zachary could do nothing but raise her up, and when he had his arms about her she clung like young ivy that has got a hold on a sapling.

The peculiar yet familiar fragrance crept into the pastor's nostrils; the lassie's beauty dazzled him, blotting out the room.

"You're ower bonny for flesh and blood," he muttered faintly.

She twined her arms round his neck; her hair, like a golden net, fell over his shoulders. The storm had ceased, and the peace was beautiful to his tired soul. Gently she drew him to the door, and as she opened it he saw again the long gold streets of Babylon, with the pale hyacinth skies above, the tinkling bells, the festoons of roses.

And now he saw that the girl in his arms wore a chaplet of white roses and a purple robe over her falling lawn.

"It's a long way to Babylon from Drumknockie," she said. "Will you not come in and rest?"

Struggling with the luxurious languor of his senses the minister glanced back into his room and saw the horned head on the table; the lips were moving in a sneer of triumph, and the long wicked eyes shot a gleam of contempt.

With a yell of horror the Rev. Zachary sprang back and snatched at the head; it was in his arms instead of the fair woman; it lay on his bosom like a bride, but his feet were still on the golden streets of Babylon, and he could not find the door into his room. The head had grown a long, dangling body now, and arms that held him fast; a pit opened in the golden street and the Rev. Zachary slipped down... down... down.

"Preserve us a'!" exclaimed old Maisie. "What for does the minister need to gang oot wi' the nicht like this?"

She sprang out of her little bedroom and into the kitchen, and then into the passage; a howl of chilly air had come into the house, then the door was clapped to.

The Rev. Zachary had gone into the darkness; the fire was nearly extinguished on the hearth, the taper was blown out, and the Bible lay on the floor.

"Losh!" cried old Maisie as she picked up the Holy Book, "nae doot he's gang on some errand o' maircy, and may a' gude attend him, but this is no the manner to sarve the blessed Word!"

They found him frozen stiff in a snowdrift on the way to the hills; dead, with neither coat nor hat, and clasped in his arms the head of the old goat that Tam Todd had hoped would pass for that of a fine Cheviot sheep.

"It's nae wonder," said old Maisie, "that the douce man should gang queer in the head wi' a' that book making an' learning, but, preserve us a'! why should he tak' wi' him the heid o' the willie goat? And he must have creppit into the kitchen maist carefu' and got it frae the basket whaur it were hid biding Tam Todd's lad. It's unco' queer, and maybe the Deil has a hand in't, but I lay the blame o' a gude man's death on Tam Todd."

RED CHAMPAGNE

When Marco Gherardi pledged his troth to Geva Gradenigo at her villa on the Brenta the oranges showed jade-green beneath the dark, glossy leaves and the July grapes, hard and bloomless, spilled from the plates of gleaming lustre ware.

Geva leant on the table with chequered light and shade of vine leaves moving over the smooth chestnut locks into which a last white rose was negligently pinned; her face was pallid as a sea-water pearl, and her two long hands lay in the warm clasp of her dark lover.

Her dress gleamed the colour of moonlight; in her heavy-lidded eyes lay tears for the beauty of the purple haze and the air drowsy with the scent of ripening fruit.

"Pledge me till death," she said, "and past death?"

"Till death and past death," he whispered, and kissed her frail fingers with long kisses, like a bee lingering by a flower.

Geva drew away her right hand and took a silver bodkin from her hair; the drooping rose fell from her locks to the table of pale marble. Delicately she raised the slim, amber-hued bottle of white wine and poured the clear drink into the two glasses of milky lines that stood beside the platters of piled grapes, then she pricked her arm and let the blood run into the glasses, drop by drop, sliding into the fragrant liquid.

Marco also lightly stabbed his wrist veins, and the mingled blood floated together as they drank the flushed wine, swearing eternal fidelity in the warm, sleepy hot, hot afternoon; yea, eternal, for their vows reached beyond death into the still blue distances of the unknown.

That night a poisonous fly from the marshes stung Geva on the opened skin and the burning malaria ran through all her limbs. After another day and night of palpitating heat Geva died in the great bed of chestnut wood with the Gradenigo coat of arms on the head-board and Marco along the bedstep with buried face; till they took away the four painted candles and the long, narrow, gilt coffin.

Then Marco wandered through the mellow autumn wooing melancholy in leafless groves, till October found him in Venice amid the first glare and clatter of Carnival.

He was caught into the stream of gaiety, of riot, of licence; beneath yellow moon and yellow lanterns, Arlequino whispered his immortal jests, Spavento rattled his sword and Tartaglia grinned. Columbina shook her gauzy plumes, and lisping murmurs from the folds of black and white *beauta* asked when the Duca Gherardi was likely to wed.

Men who had forgotten Geva Gradenigo, and women who had never known her, mocked him for his sad face and sullen movements, till the music and the light balloons, the pennons against the autumn sky, the fantastic crowd on the Piazza, the languorous couples passing in the cushioned gondolas, the doves flying above the bronze horses of San Marco into the wine-purple air filled with the powdered gold of Carnival dust, worked their way with him. When the first shuddering chill of winter sent the freezing waves over the sun-withered seaweed of the palace steps Marco was betrothed to Camilla Andreini, and in Carnival time the marriage feasts began.

Scaramouche, with his guitar, danced behind the wedding procession, and the music of Furlanetto was played in the rococo ballroom, where the Murano candelabra glanced with rainbow colours and the masquers ran in and mingled with the guests.

Brilliant as a pearl in cloth of silver, with flowing veils of black lace and a bouquet of diamonds, the bride danced a gavotte with the bridegroom; the violins played the "Devil's Sonata," that inhuman music that Tartini heard in a dream; the blonde and happy light illuminated a company gay as sunshine on a stream, only Camilla whispered to her husband during the measures of the dance: "Who is the mask clothed like me in cloth of silver and priceless lace?"

Marco glanced where this lady sat alone and did not know who she might be.

"See," added Camilla, "she, too, has a bouquet of diamonds, and I did not know that there was another in Venice!"

Marco was also amazed to see the second bouquet of diamonds lying before the masked lady on her table, but when the dance was over he drew from his saffron waistcoat a single eight-sided sapphire.

"This is unique," he said, "the heirloom of our house. Ask her who she is!" he cried; but before they could reach the mask she had disappeared, and in the voluptuous melodies of the violins, in the tender smiles of the women, the murmurs of the men, the feast danced through the limpid, frosty hours of night.

Now the bride was led to the doors of the nuptial chamber, and guests and masks alike charged their glasses with bubbling champagne of France. The doors closed behind the bridal couple and the glasses were raised...

"But my wine is red!" cried one. "And mine!" another. "And mine!" a third. "The colour of blood!" screamed a woman.

And as they gazed Camilla ran in from the balcony.

"Did you not go with Marco into the bridal chamber?" asked the pale mother.

"Nay, I was on the balcony listening to the concert over the water—"

"Who went into the bedchamber with the Duca Gherardi?" asked the guests, and pale as snow they looked at each other above the goblets of red champagne.

The air blew very chill from the sea and they all were silent as if something passed through the room and out by the grand entrance, then they rushed and broke open the bedchamber door; there was no bride, but on the bridal couch lay Marco Gherardi dead, and staining the white velvet coverlet was blood, for all his wrist veins had been opened by a silver bodkin, such as women use to pin their hair.

THE SIGN-PAINTER AND THE CRYSTAL FISHES

I. THE RIVER AND THE HOUSE

The house was built beside a river. In the evening the sun would lie reflected in the dark water, a stain of red in between the thick shadows cast by the buildings. It was twilight now, and there was the long ripple of dull crimson, shifting as the water rippled sullenly between the high houses.

Beneath this house was an old stake, hung at the bottom with stagnant green, white and dry at the top. A rotting boat that fluttered the tattered remains of faded crimson cushions was affixed to the stake by a fraying rope. Sometimes the boat was thrown against the post by the strong evil ripples, and there was a dismal creaking noise.

Opposite this house was a garden—a narrow strip of ground closed round by the blank, dark houses, and led up to from the water by a flight of crumbling steps.

Nothing grew in this garden but tall, bright, rank grass and a small tree that bore white flowers. The house it belonged to was empty and shuttered; so was every house along the canal except this one, at the top window of which Lucius Cranfield sat shivering in his mean red coat. He was biting his finger and looking out across the water at the tree with pale flowers knocking at the closed shutter beside it.

The room was bare and falling to decay. Cobwebs swung from the great beam in the roof, and in every corner a spider's web was spun across the dirty plaster walls.

There was no glass in the window, and the shutters swung loose on broken hinges. Now and again they creaked against the flat brick front of the house, and then Lucius Cranfield winced.

He held a round, clear mirror in his hand, and sometimes he looked away from the solitary tree to glance into it. When he did so he beheld a pallid face surrounded with straight brown hair, lips that had once been beautiful, and blurred eyes veined with red like some curious stone.

As the red sunlight began to grow fainter in the water a step sounded on the rotting stairway, the useless splitting door was pushed open, and Lord James Fontaine entered.

Slowly, and with a mincing step, he came across the dusty floor. He wore a dress of bright violet watered silk, his hair was rolled fantastically, and powdered such a pure white that his face looked sallow by contrast. To remedy this he had painted his cheeks and his lips, and powdered his forehead and chin. But the impression made was not of a pink and fresh complexion, but of a yellow countenance rouged. There were long pearls in his ears and under his left eye an enormous patch. His eyes slanted towards his nose, his nostrils curved upwards, and his thin lips were smiling.

He carried a cane hung with blood-coloured tassels, and his waistcoat was embroidered with green flowers, the hue of an emerald, and green flowers the tint of a pale sea.

"You paint signs, do you not?" he said, and nodded.

"Yes, I paint signs," answered the other. He looked away from Lord James and across the darkening water at the lonely tree opposite. The sky above the deserted houses was turning a cold wet grey. A flight of crows went past, clung for a moment round the chimney-pots, and flew on again.

"Will you design *me* a sign-board?" asked Lord James, smiling. "Something noble and gay, for I have taken a new house in town."

"My workshop is downstairs," said Lucius Cranfield, without looking round. "Why did you come up?" He laid down the mirror and rubbed his cold fingers together.

"I rang and there was no answer, I knocked and there was no answer, so I pushed open the door and came up; why not?" Lord James regarded the sign-painter keenly, and smiled again, and pressed the knob of his clouded cane against his chin.

"Oh, why not?" echoed Lucius Cranfield. "Only this is a poor place to come to for a gay and noble sign."

He turned his head now, and there was a curious twist on his colourless lips.

"But you have a very splendid painting swinging outside your own door," said Lord James suavely. "Never did I see fairer drawing nor brighter hues. It is your work?" he questioned.

"Mine, yes," assented the sign-painter drearily.

"Fashion me a sign-board such as that," said Lord James. Lucius Cranfield left off rubbing his hands together.

"The same subjects?" he asked.

The other lowered his lids.

"The subjects are curious," he replied. "Where did you get them?"

"From life," said the sign-painter, staring at the tattered veils of cobwebs fluttering on the broken window-frame. "From my life."

The bright dark eyes of the visitor flickered from right to left. He moved a little nearer the window, where, despite the thickening twilight, his violet silk coat gleamed like the light on a sheet of water.

"You have had a strange life," he remarked, sneering, "to cull from it such incidents."

"What did you behold that was so extraordinary?" asked Lucius Cranfield.

"On one side there is depicted a gallows, a man in a gay habit hanging on it, and his face has some semblance to your own; the reverse bears the image of a fish, white, yet shot with all the colours... it is so skilfully executed that it looks as if it moved through the water..."

An expression of faint and troubled interest came over the sign-painter's face.

"Have you ever seen such a fish?" he asked.

Lord James's features seemed to contract and sharpen.

"Never," he said hastily.

Lucius Cranfield rose slowly and stiffly.

"There are two in the world," he said, half to himself; "and before the end I shall find the other, and then everything will be mended and put straight."

"Unless you lose your own token first," remarked Lord James harshly.

"How did you know I had one?" asked the sign-painter sharply.

Lord James laughed.

"Oh, you're going mad, my fine friend! Do you not feel that you must be, living alone in such fashion in this old house?" Lucius Cranfield dragged himself to a cupboard in the wall.

"How my limbs ache!" he muttered. "Mad?" A look of cunning spread over his features. "No, I shall not go mad while I have the one crystal fish, nor before I find the owner of the other."

It was so dark they could barely see each other; but the nobleman's dress still shone bright and cold in the gloom.

"Yet it is enough to make a man go mad," he remarked suavely, "to reflect how rich and handsome you were once, with what fine clothes and furniture and friends... and then to remember how your father was hanged, and you were ruined, and all through the lies of your enemy...

"But my enemy died, too," said Lucius Cranfield. He took a thick candle and a rusty tinder-box out of the cupboard.

"His son is alive," replied Lord James.

A coarse yellow flame spurted across the dust.

"I wish I had killed them both," said the sign-painter; "but I could never find the son... How badly the candle burns!..."

He held the tinder to the cold wax, and only a small tongue of feeble fire sprang up.

"You are quite mad!" smiled Lord James. "You never killed either... and now that your blood is chilled with misery and weakened with evil days, you never will."

The candle-flame strengthened and illumined the chamber. It showed Lord James holding his sharp chin in a long white hand, and woke his diamonds into stars.

"Will you come downstairs and choose your design?" said Lucius Cranfield, shivering. "Take care of the stairs. They are rather dusty."

He shuffled to the door and held aloft the light. It revealed the twisting stairway where the plaster hung cracked and dry on the walls, or bulged damp and green in patches as the damp had come through. The rafters were warped and bending, and in one spot a fan-shaped fungus had spread in a blotch of mottled orange.

Lord James came softly up behind the sign-painter, and peered over the stairs.

"This is a mean place," he said, smiling, "for a great gentleman to live in... and you were a great gentleman once, Mr. Cranfield."

The other gave him a cunning look over his shoulder.

"When I find the owner of the fish," he answered, "I shall be a great gentleman again or kill my enemy—that is in the spell."

They went downstairs slowly because of the rotting steps and uncertain light. Lord James rested his long fingers lightly on the dusty balustrade.

"Do you not find the days very long and dull here?" he asked.

The reply came unsteadily from the bowed red figure of the sign-painter.

"No... I paint... and then I make umbrellas."

"Umbrellas!" Lord James laughed unpleasantly.

"And parasols. Would you not like a parasol for your wife, James Fontaine?"

"Ah, you know me, it seems."

"I know what you call yourself," said Lucius Cranfield. "And here is my studio. Will you look at the designs upon the wall?"

Lord James grinned and stepped delicately along the dark passage to the door indicated. It opened into a low chamber the entire depth of the house. There were windows on either side: one way looking onto the river, the other onto the street.

Lucius Cranfield set the candle in a green bottle on the table, and pointed round the walls where all manner of drawings on canvas, wood, and paper hung. They depicted horrible and fantastic things—mandrakes, dragons, curious shells and plants, monsters, and distorted flowers. In one corner were a number of parasols of silk and brocade, ruffled and frilled, having carved handles and ribboned sticks.

Lord James put up his glass and looked about him.

"So you know who I am?" he said, speaking in an absorbed way and keeping his back to Lucius Cranfield, who stood huddled together on the other side of the table, staring before him with dead-seeming eyes.

There was no answer, and Lord James laughed softly.

"You paint very well, Mr. Cranfield, but I must have something more cheerful than any of these"—he pointed his elegant cane at the designs. "That fish, now, that you have on your own sign, that is a beautiful thing."

The sign-painter groaned and thrust his fingers into his untidy brown hair.

"I cannot paint that again," he said.

"Sell me the sign, then." Lord James spoke quickly.

"I cannot... it is hanging there that it may be seen... that whosoever holds the other fish may see it... and then..."

"How mad you are!" cried Lord James. "What then, even should one come who has the other fish?" His black eyes blinked sharply, and his lips twitched back from his teeth.

"Then I shall find my enemy. The witch said so..."

"But you may die first."

"I cannot die till the spell is accomplished," shivered Lucius Cranfield. "Nor can I lose the fish."

Lord James put his hand to his waistcoat-pocket.

"Your light is very dim," he remarked. "I do not see clearly, but I think I observe a violet-coloured parasol—"

The other lifted his head.

"They are very interesting to make."

"Will you show me that one?"

Lucius Cranfield turned slowly towards the far corner of the room.

"I began to work on that the night my father was hanged... as I sewed on the frills I thought of my enemies and how I hated them; and the night I killed one of them I finished it, carving the handle into the likeness of an ivory rose."

"You have sinned also," said Lord James, through his teeth. He took his hand from his pocket and put it behind his back. "I have been a great sinner," answered the sign-painter.

He took the purple parasol from the corner and shook out its shimmering silk furbelows.

"I will buy that." Lord James leant against the table, close to the candle flaring in the green bottle. In its yellow light the brilliant colour of his coat shone like a jewel.

"The parasol is not for sale," said Lucius Cranfield sourly, gazing down on it. "Why do you not choose your design and go?" Now it was quite dark, both outside, beyond the windows, and in the corners of the long room. The waters sounded insistently as they lapped against the house. There was no moon; but through a rift in the thick, murky sky one star flickered, and the sign-painter lifted his dimmed eyes from the candle-flame and looked at it.

"What do you see?" asked Lord James curiously. He came softly up bed the other.

"A star," was the reply. "It is shining above the lonely white tree that is always knocking at the closed shutters..."

Lord James's hand came round from behind his back.

"But one can never see them both at the same time," continued the sign-painter. "When the star comes out, the tree is hidden; and only when the star sets..."

Lord James's fine hand rose slowly and fell swiftly...

Lucius Cranfield sank on his face silently, and the flaring light of the unsnuffed candle glistened on the wet dagger as it was withdrawn from between his shoulders.

Lord James stepped back and gazed with a long smile at his victim, who writhed an instant and then lay still on the dusty floor.

The sound of the water without seemed to increase his strength. The secretive yet turbulent noise of it filled the chamber like a presence as Lord James turned over the body of the sign-painter and opened his red coat.

In an inner pocket he found it, wrapped in a piece of blue satin.

The crystal fish. It was of all colours yet of no colour; translucent as water, holding, like a bubble, all hues, finely wrought with fins and scales, light and cold to the hand, shining with a pure light of its own to the eye.

Lord James rose from his knees and put out the candle.

The river sounded so loud that he paused to listen to it. He thought he could distinguish the swish of oars and the latter of them in the rowlocks.

He went to the window and looked out. By the glimmer of the star and the radiance cast by the fish in his hand he could discern that there was nobody on the river, only the deserted boat fastened to the rotting stake.

He smiled; the faint light was caught in his ribbons, his diamonds, his dark, evil eyes. As he stared up and down the black road of water, the crystal fish began to writhe in his hand. It pushed and struggled, then leapt through his fingers and plunged into the blackness of the river.

Lord James peered savagely after it, his smile changing to a grin of anger. But the fish had sunk like a bolt of iron, and thinking of the depth of the river Lord James was comforted.

He came back to the table. It was quite dark, but his eyes served him equally well day or night. He picked up his clouded cane with the crimson tassels, his black hat laced with gold, his vivid green cloak, he kissed his hand to the prone body of the sign-painter, and left the room. In a leisurely fashion he walked down the passage, pushed open the crazy front door, and stepped out into the lonely street.

He looked up at the sign on which were painted the crystal fish and the man on the gallows; then he began to put on his gloves.

As he did so the violet parasol came to his mind. He turned back.

Softly he re-entered the long studio. The noise of the water had subsided to a mere murmur. Rats were running about the room and sitting on the body of Lucius Cranfield. He could see them despite the intense darkness, and he stepped delicately to avoid their tails.

The violet parasol was on the floor near the dead man. He stooped to pick it up, and the rats squealed and showed their teeth.

Lord James nodded to them and left the house again with the parasol under his arm.

THE SIGN-PAINTER AND THE CRYSTAL FISHES

II. THE RIVER AND THE GARDEN

The garden sloped down to the straight high-road upon the side to which the house faced, and at the back ran the river dividing the pleasaunce from the meadows.

Separating the garden from the road was a prim box hedge, very high, very wide, and very old. Behind this grew the neat garden flowers, and beneath it the tangled weeds that edged the road.

Here sat Lord James on a milestone, playing Faro with a one-eyed gipsy.

The summer sunset sparkled on the red gables of the house and in the clothes of Lord James, which were of crimson and blue sarcenet branched with gold and silver.

The gipsy was young and ugly; he wore a green patch over his eyeless socket, and now and then listened, keenly, to the sound of the church-bells that came up from the valley, for the village ringers were practising for Lord James's wedding.

The two played silently. The red and black cards scattered over the close green grass shaded by the large wild-parsley flowers. Beside the milestone lay Lord James's hat, stick, and cloak. His horse was fastened by its bridle to a stout branch of a laurel-tree that bent over from the garden.

"You always win," said the gipsy.

Lord James smiled, then coughed till he shook the powder off his face on to his cravat.

"Another game," he said, and shuffled the cards.

At this a lady looked over the box hedge, and gave them both a bitter frown.

Little bright pink and blue ribbons were threaded through her high-piled white curls, round her neck was a diamond necklace, and on the front of her black velvet bodice a long trail of jasmine was pinned. Her painted lips curled scornfully, and her azure eyes darkened as she stared across and over the box hedge at Lord James.

He looked up at her, waved his hand, and rose.

"You are late," she remarked stiffly.

"I have been playing cards," he answered. "May I present you to my friend?" He pointed to the gipsy.

"No," she said, and turned her back.

The gipsy laughed silently. The sound of the bells swelled and receded in the golden evening.

"Take my horse round to the stables." Lord James grinned at the gipsy, and gathered up his hat and cloak from the grass.

"I hate those bells!" cried the lady pettishly.

"They will ring no more after tomorrow, my dear."

Lord James came round to the gate as he spoke, and entered the garden.

She gave him a side-glance, and pouted. Her enormous pink silk hoop, draped with festoons of white roses, overspread the narrow garden-path, and crushed the southernwood that edged it. Her hands rested on her black velvet panniers embroidered with garlands of crimson carnations. There was a moon-shaped patch on her bare throat and one like a star on her rouged cheek; beneath her short skirts showed her black buckle shoes and immensely high red heels. Her name was Serena Thornton.

"I have broken my parasol," she said, looking at the gables of her house where the red-gold sunset rested. "The violet one you brought me."

"It can be mended," answered Lord James.

He came up to her, and they kissed.

"Yes," assented Serena. "I sent it to be mended today," she added. He laughed.

"There is no one here can mend a parasol like that. You must give it to me, Serena, and I will take it to town."

They moved slowly along the gravel walk, he in front of her, since her hoop did not allow him to be by her side.

It was a very pleasant garden. There were beds of pinks, of stocks, of roses, bushes of laurel, yew, and box, all intersected with little paths that crossed one another and led towards the house.

"There is a man in the village," said Lady Serena, "who is a maker of umbrellas. He came here yesterday."

"Ah?" questioned Lord James. He glanced back over his shoulder. "I heard he was painting a new sign for 'The Goat and Compasses,' and that he had made a beautiful blue umbrella for the host, so I sent down my parasol."

A slight greenish tinge, visible through the paint and powder, overspread Lord James's handsome face.

"It was careless of you to break it," he said softly.

Lady Serena lifted her shoulders.

"I could not help it. Shall I tell you how it happened?"

They had reached a square plot of close grass round which ran the box hedge and a low stone coping. In the centre stood a prim fountain, and in its clear water swam the golden and ruby carp.

"Yes, tell me how it happened," said Lord James. He pressed his handkerchief to his thin lips and looked up at the sunset.

"I wish they would stop those bells!" cried Lady Serena.

"They are practising for our wedding tomorrow, my dear," he smiled.

They could walk now side by side, she looking in front of her, and he gazing at the sunset that was pale and bright, the colour of soft gold, of pink coral, and of a dove's wings above the gables of her house.

"I was walking by the river two days ago," said Lady Serena, "and I had in my hand the crystal fish. Do you remember, Lord James, that I showed it to you just before you left for town?"

"Yes; a foolish toy," he answered.

"How pleasant the box smells!" murmured Lady Serena, in a softer tone. "Well, I walked along the bank, thinking of you, and as I looked into the water I saw another fish—it floated just as if it were swimming—and oh, it was like the one I held in my hand! Just as it neared me it became entangled in the water weeds..."

"This does not explain how you broke your parasol," remarked Lord James.

"I drew the fish to land with it—my new parasol that your little black boy had just brought me—and broke the handle."

Lord James turned his pallid face towards her.

"Did you get the fish?"

"Yes. It is just like the one I have." She pulled out a green ribbon from the white velvet bag that hung on her arm, and at the end of it dangled two crystal fishes, cut and carved finely, holding a clear light, and filled with changing colours.

Lady Serena touched one with her scented forefinger. "That is the one I found. See, it has a bright blood-like stain across the side."

"So it has," said Lord James, putting up his glass. "It is curious you should have found it. A witch gave you the other, did you not say?"

"Yes," she answered half sullenly. "And she told me that the other was owned by my lover, and that he must live in misery till he found me." She turned the blue light of her eyes on her companion. "*You* should have had it," she said, and slipped the fishes back into her bag.

The afterglow was fading from the sky, and they turned towards the house.

"I won three thousand pounds at Faro last night," said Lord James, "and I have brought you some presents."

And he thrust his hand into his pocket and drew out a string of amethysts.

"I dislike the colour," said Lady Serena, and put it aside. "It is the colour you wear," he answered.

She took the necklace at this with a sudden laugh, and fastened it round her long, pale throat.

They reached the three shallow steps that led to the open door of the house, and passed side by side out of the sunset glow into the soft-hued gloom of the wide hall.

In the great banqueting-room a dinner of two covers was laid. The service was of agate and silver, the glasses twisted with milk-white lines. The table was lit by six tall candles painted with wreaths of pinks and forget-me-nots, and their light ran gleaming and faint over the white cloth.

"I am going to try on my wedding-dress," said Lady Serena. "Will you wait for me?"

"It is unlucky to wear your wedding-dress before your wedding-day," answered Lord James.

But she left the chamber without a word or a smile.

The room opened by wide windows onto the terrace at the back that sloped down to the river, and the sound of the water throbbing between its banks seemed to grow in volume and to speak threateningly to Lord James as he sat at the table with the glass and silver glittering before him, and the heart-shaped candle-flames casting a flickering glow over his sickly face.

It was the same river, and he knew it. As the last flush of light faded from the heavens he could see the moon, a strong pearl colour, rise above the trees, and a great sparkling reflection fell across the river, marking with lines of silver the turbulent eddies that chased one another down the stream.

After a while Lord James rose and walked softly to the window, and his eyes became wide and bright as he stroked his chin and stared at the river.

When he turned round again, Lucius Cranfield stood in the doorway looking at him.

A spasm of fear contracted Lord James's features; then he spoke evenly.

"Good evening," he said.

"Good evening," replied Lucius Cranfield, and he bowed. "I have brought back a parasol I have mended—a lady's parasol, purple, with an ivory rose on the handle."

Between them was an ill-lit space of room and the bright table bearing the candles. They looked at each other, and Lord James's face grew long and foxy.

"How much do I owe you, Mr. Cranfield?" he asked.

"A great deal," said the sign-painter, shaking his head. "Oh, a great deal!"

THE SIGN-PAINTER AND THE CRYSTAL FISHES

Smiling, he set the parasol against a chair. His eyes were no longer bloodshot nor his cheeks pallid. His hair was neatly dressed. He wore the same red suit, and between the shoulder-blades it had been slit and mended with stitchings of gold thread.

"How much?" repeated Lord James.

Lucius Cranfield laughed.

"I do not believe that you are alive at all," sneered the other, rubbing his hands together. "How did you get away from the rats?"

"Do you hear the river?" whispered the sign-painter. "It is the same river."

Lord James came towards the table.

"I will pay you tomorrow for your work," and he pointed to the mended parasol.

"That is no debt of yours," answered Lucius Cranfield. "I did it for the lady of the house, Serena Thornton."

"She is my betrothed," said Lord James. "And I will pay you tomorrow—"

"No... tonight."

And the sign-painter smiled and stepped nearer.

"You lost the crystal fish," murmured Lord James, biting his forefinger and glancing round the dark, lonely room.

"But someone else has found it."

The other gave a snarl of rage.

"No! It is at the bottom of the river!"

At that Lucius Cranfield leant forward and seized his enemy by the throat. Lord James shrieked, and they swayed together for a moment. But the sign-painter twisted the other's head round on his shoulders and dropped him, a heap of gay clothes, on the waxed floor.

Then he began to sing, and turned to the open window.

The river was quiet now, flowing peacefully in between its banks, and Lucius Cranfield stepped out onto the terrace and walked towards its waters shining in the moonlight.

Almost before the last echo of his footsteps had died away in the silent room, Lady Serena Thornton entered, holding her dress up from her shoes.

Her gown was white, all wreathed across the hoop with ropes of seed-pearls, and laced across the bodice with diamonds. In her high head-dress floated two soft plumes fastened with clusters of pale roses. Round her neck hung Lord James's gift of amethysts.

She stood in the doorway, her painted lips parted, her dark blue eyes fixed on the body of her betrothed husband.

Presently she went up and looked at him; then she sat down on the chair by the table—sat down, breathing heavily—with her right hand on the smooth satin of her bodice, and slow, strange changes passing over her face. She glanced at the purple parasol, resting across the chair where Lord James should have sat, and then out at the distant river, that showed white as her bridal-dress where the moonlight caught its ripples.

She heard the far-off singing of the sign-painter, and she sighed, closing her eyes.

The six candles burnt steadily, casting a rim of dark shadow round the table and the dead man on the floor, and glittering in the embroidered flowers on his gaudy coat and in the jewels of the woman at the table.

The black clock on the mantelshelf struck ten. The sound was echoed by the chimes from the village church.

Lady Serena Thornton rose and went upstairs, her wide hoop brushing the balustrade either side, her high heels tapping on the polished wood.

She entered her room and lit a little silver lamp on the dressing-table.

The chamber looked out upon the back; the window was open, and she could still see the river and hear Lucius Cranfield singing.

Slowly she took the feathers, ribbons and flowers out of her curls, and laid them on the tulip-wood table. Then she shook down her hair from its wire frame and brushed the powder out of it. She had almost forgotten what colour it was—in reality a ruby golden-brown, like the tint of wallflowers.

She unlaced her bodice and flung aside her jewels. She stepped out of her hoop and took off her satin coat, staring at herself in the gilt oval mirror.

Then she washed her face free of paint and powder in her gold basin, and tied up her locks with a red ribbon. She cast off her long earrings, her bracelets, her rings, the necklace Lord James had given her. This slipped, like a glitter of purple water, through her fingers, and shone in a little heap of stars on the gleaming waxed floor.

She arrayed herself in a brown dress, plain and straight, and took the two fishes from their velvet bag to hang them round her neck. Again she looked at herself. Who would have known her? Not Lord James himself, could he have risen from the floor in the solitary room below, and come up the wide stairs to gaze at her. Her face was utterly changed, her carriage different.

She blew out the lamp. A faint trail of smoke stained the moonlight that filled the room. She listened and heard the river and the sign-painter singing. On her bosom the fishes throbbed and glowed, opal-coloured and luminous.

Leaving the room lightly, softly she descended through the dark to the dining-room.

The six flower-wreathed candles still burnt steadily among the glass and silver. She glanced at Lord James sorrowfully, and picked up the mended parasol.

As she did so the bells broke out in a volume of glad sound—the villagers practising yet again for her wedding on the morrow.

Lady Serena Thornton smiled, and as Lucius Cranfield had done, and almost in his steps, went down the long room and through the open window on to the terrace. Slowly she walked towards the river, which she could see moving restlessly under the moonlight. The bells were very loud, but through them came the words of his song—

> "The clouds were tangled in the trees—
>   They broke the boughs and spoiled the fruit;
> The sleeper knows what the sleeper sees—
>   You play spades, and I follow suit!
>
> The clouds came down the drops of rain,
>   And woke the grass to blooms of fire;
> The sleeper tore his dream in twain,
>   And sought for the cards in the bitter mire!"

The bells ceased suddenly. Lady Serena saw the dark figure of the sign-painter, standing at the edge of the water, his back to her.

"If I have won, 'tis little matter;
    If I have lost, 'tis naught at all;
The wind will chill and the sun will flatter,
    And the damp earth fill the mouth of all."

There was a boat before him, rocking on the argent water, and as the lady came up the sign-painter stooped over it. Then he turned and saw her.

"Good even," said Lady Serena. He took her hands and kissed her face. The sound of the river was heavily in their ears.

"I found your fish," she whispered.

He nodded, and they entered the boat. It was lined with violet silk and scented with spices.

"The villagers will have practised for nothing," said Lady Serena. Lucius Cranfield loosened the rope that held the boat fast to a willow, and it began to drift down the stream towards the town.

"We are going to a house where a tree with white flowers knocks for admittance on the shutters," he said.

"I know," she answered; "I know."

She sat opposite to him, leaning back, and the light night wind blew apart her brown robe here and there on the gleam of the bright green petticoat beneath. Her yellow hair floated behind her, and the crystal fishes rose and fell with her breathing. Across her knees lay the purple parasol.

They looked at each other and smiled with parted lips. The boat sped swiftly under a high bank, treeless and full under the rays of the moon. Here, by a round stone, sat two figures playing cards.

Lucius Cranfield glanced up. The players turned white, grinning faces down towards the boat. They were the one-eyed gipsy and Lord James.

"Good night," nodded the sign-painter. "I do not believe you are alive at all. Why, I can almost see through you!..."

"Do you know me?" mocked Lady Serena.

And the boat was swept away along the winding river.

Lord James listened to the sign-painter's song that floated up from the dark water.

> "If I win, 'tis little matter;
>   If I lose, 'tis naught at all;
> The wind will chill and the sun will flatter,
>   And the red earth stop the mouths of all."

"They will never get there," grinned Lord James. "I shall go down tomorrow and see the empty boat upside down, tossing outside the shuttered house."

"There is no tomorrow for such as you," leered the gipsy. "You had your neck broken an hour ago... presently we will go home... your deal..."

Lord James sighed, and a great cloud suddenly overspread the moon.

The gipsy began to sing in a harsh voice, and his eyes turned red in his head as he shuffled the cards.

> "If I win, 'tis little matter;
>   If I lose, 'tis naught at all;
> The wind will chill and the sun will flatter,
>   And the damp earth stop the mouths of all."

Far away down the river the boat flashed for the last time in the moonlight, then was lost to sight under the shadow of the overhanging trees.

ALSO AVAILABLE
BY THE SAME AUTHOR

*It was nearly dark in the cloisters; Lally looked up
at the boar's head, grotesque in the dimness.
"A strange thing to carve in a Christian church," he thought.*

Following a romantic scandal in the Duke's court, Lally Duchene is dismissed to a new post at a monastery turned asylum nestled in the wine country of the Rhineland. Unfazed by local superstitions about ghosts and nixies in the forests, his days slip by in a haze.

But something is stirring in this woodland idyll. Among the patients is a woman possessing an otherworldly aura. Phantasms disturb the night, and the vestiges of a sinister paganism leer from beneath holy facades. As the wine harvest approaches and Lally's past catches up with him at the monastery, eternal forces are awakening—and a carnage of ancient rites draws near.

First published in 1921, this full-bodied tale of mythical weirdness in nineteenth-century Germany is a vintage to be savoured.

ALSO AVAILABLE

*"Love will have its sacrifices.
No sacrifice without blood. Let us go to sleep now."*

A prophecy threatens a volcanic upheaval for a star-crossed pair. A forbidden rite binds a dark arts dabbler to a phantom bride. A barstool chancer invites a devilish retribution on the dance floor.

Beckoning from this tome are twelve tales of dark romance and undying passions hailing from 1832 to 2022, marrying bewitching classics by Mary Shelley, Wilkie Collins and Angela Carter with twisting modern pieces by Nalo Hopkinson, Tracy Fahey and V. Castro—alongside the classic Gothic novella of sapphic vampire romance *Carmilla*. Indulging in the strangest eddies of literary love, this new anthology bids you enter a doom-laden yet irresistibly seductive corner of the Weird.

For more Tales of the Weird titles
visit the British Library Shop (shop.bl.uk)

We welcome any suggestions, corrections or feedback you may have,
and will aim to respond to all items addressed to the following:

The Editor (Tales of the Weird), British Library Publishing,
The British Library, 96 Euston Road, London NW1 2DB

We also welcome enquiries through our Twitter account, @BL_Publishing.